THE
FATAL
MIND

A NOVEL

THE
FATAL
MIND

A NOVEL

N.J. GALLEGOS

WINDING ROAD STORIES

NEW YORK | LOS ANGELES

Jacket design by Rejenne Pavon

Jacket Copyright © 2024 by Winding Road Stories

Interior Design by Winding Road Stories

ISBN#: 978-1-960724-30-4 (pbk)
ISBN#: 978-1-960724-31-1 (ebook)

Published by Winding Road Stories

www.windingroadstories.com

1

M RS. COMBS CLIMBED ABOARD her yellow noble steed: the Number 9 school bus. Twice daily—at 7 a.m. and 3:30 p.m.—she started her route, making her way from the bus barn and through town until fields and dirt lined the road. Into what the folks living within city limits called: *The Sticks*. Potatoes, barley, and alfalfa sprouted from rich dirt—sold for a tidy profit assuming farmers weren't hit with blight, drought, or hail.

She found farm kids—she considered every kid living out here a farm kid, even if they didn't reside on an actual farm—were far more polite than snotty city kids who glorified in being absolute booger snots. City kids were little jerks who tossed spit balls, seat hopped when the bus was in motion, and God, they had horrible potty mouths; delighting in screaming curse words and dissolving into giggles when her stern gaze flitted to the mirror.

In her younger years, she'd been staunchly pro-life, voting the straight Republican ticket. Too many years driving the city route exposed her to the truth of life, and she now supported Roe v. Wade wholeheartedly. Kids could be awful, especially nowadays with social media. They endlessly tormented each other, unable to escape even in the safety of their own homes thanks to the constant influx of bullying aided by technology.

But, as much as she bitched to her friends about the kids—she enjoyed her work. More these days since she was off the city route. She loved guiding her bus down well-worn roads. Enjoyed watching good kids grow up and develop their own interests. Hell, she even liked stopping at railroads and opening the door, listening for train whistles while the scent of fresh cut crops wafted inside. It was an orderly job and she craved routine. Morning: pick up the rug rats and drop them at school. Afternoon: fetch them from school and back home they went. It had a lovely symmetry to it, and she felt like she was making a difference. Helping mold the youth of America—The Future; whether she liked it or not—even if all she did was drive a school bus.

Sadly, her charges this year were more challenging than ever, the booger snots outnumbering the good kids 2:1.

"Hi, Mrs. Combs!" said gap-toothed Marilee as she bounded up the steps. She was one of nice ones.

Mrs. Combs smiled. "Hi yourself, Marilee."

Marilee's brother followed sullenly, looking like someone pissed in his Wheaties.

"Hi, Dustin."

"Hi," Dustin mumbled, hands buried in pockets. Head hung down. Involuntarily, Mrs. Combs took in his face and forearms—looking for telltale bruises or scrapes. Their Pop had a nasty habit of talking with his fists, or at least, that was the gossip down at the beauty salon. Seeing none, she breathed a sigh of relief and pulled the door shut.

A bright flash of sunlight reflected from the mirror into her eyes, sending an electric bolt of pain through her skull and on its heels—an irrational anger. There. Then gone. Only a second of discomfort—thinly layered rage that quickly dissipated to the dusty corners of her mind—but sweat beaded on her forehead at the stark reminder of what her life used to be like: a 24/7 headache that never took vacations, holidays, or ironically, sick days.

As a young woman, she suffered the typical pains: neck tension and the odd dull ache when she didn't get enough sleep. Nothing big. Manageable. Then menopause reared its ugly head, taking away her periods—a blessing since she bled like a stuck pig—but leaving something worse in their place.

Migraines.

But that wasn't what was happening today, was it? No. Just a blast of blinding light—nothing more. A tendril of irritation at the assault on her retinas; totally understandable. She shifted into drive and continued down the dirt road, a rooster tail of dust following her chariot as she gained speed. Normally, the kids were quiet in the morning—still reeling from being rousted from cozy beds—but excited chatter abounded today. Straining her ears, Mrs. Combs realized why: a class trip to the college planetarium. A crowd favorite each year, not that she could enjoy it. Craning her neck with eyes on an artificial sky induced vertigo the one time she'd gone. She wouldn't make that mistake again, not relishing a date with a toilet and cold bathroom floor.

"Do you think we'll get to see all the constellations?" Marilee asked hopefully. "My mom showed me Orion's Belt and the Big Dipper last night."

Chad nodded his head with the exuberance of a dog shaking water free from his coat. "Yup! We'll see all the planets and everything. Mike told me."

"I really hope we see Uranus!" Jonathan called out, wearing a broad shit-eating grin Mrs. Combs spied in the rearview mirror. He erupted into braying laughter at his own wit.

"Jonathan don't be rude," Mrs. Combs called out. Pressure bloomed behind her left eye, throbbing in time with the noise. What an awful... fucking laugh. She clenched her jaw and ground her teeth until they squeaked. The dusting of freckles on Jonathan's nose and cheeks beckoned; a good whack and he'd straighten right up. Parents these days were too soft sometimes. Not that she advocated beating, but a good spanking never hurt nobody. Her bony hand itched as she imagined the sharp snap his skin would make under her palm. Behind Coke bottle thick glasses, her light gray eyes narrowed.

Aware she was always watching, Jonathan—with great effort—stifled the guffaws spilling out of him. "Sorry Mrs. Combs." He hung his head like a beleaguered dog: *boo hoo, feel sorry for me.* He needed a swift kick in the britches. She curtly nodded to Jonathan's reflection and pressed her lips into a thin line. When she got back to the bus barn, she needed a heaping cup—no, a pot—of coffee. Caffeine cleared the cobwebs out and decluttered the brain.

Since when do you have cobwebs? she thought, chasing the thought away at once. No cobwebs. No clutter. No headaches. No spells where memories spilled from her head like someone took a melon baller and systemically went at her brain. None of that. Not since the chip. Things used to be so... awful. Life a slog filled with unrelenting agony—a thunderstorm constantly roiling between her ears, inside her skull.

White checked lines on the road bled together as she remembered. After suffering for weeks with an unrelenting headache that pained her even in sleep, she'd finally caved and booked an appointment with her family doctor, Dr. Brooks. He examined her with clinical detachment; indifferent fingertips prodding her jawline, peering into various orifices with a scope—thankfully not into her nether regions—and he'd made her perform tasks that filled her with embarrassment. Spell WORLD backwards. Draw a clock. Count backwards from 100 by seven—a task that proved more difficult than expected, filling her with anxiety. Dr. Brooks held up objects and with inquisitive eyes, waited for Mrs. Combs to name them: pen, watch, cellphone. Having completed all the doctor's tasks, she sat on the exam room table, gazing at the various medical posters tacked on the wall and awaited the verdict. What would it be? A brain tumor? One of those horrible diseases that reduced people to breathing vegetables? Lead poisoning? Had the kids on her bus finally driven her crazy—their constant noise and shenanigans causing a permanent headache to take up residence?

Dr. Brooks sat on his rolling chair, furiously jotting something down that she couldn't make out. The doctor's handwriting was sharp, sloping, nearly indecipherable—perfect for a physician.

Arms prickled with goosebumps, Mrs. Combs cleared her throat, momentarily feeling guilty about breaking the silence. "So... what's wrong with me? Is it a tumor? Cancer?" Her voice caught on the word *tumor* and her throat tightened. Thoughts of brilliantly colored bags filled with chemotherapy drugs dripping into the crook of her arm filled her mind. Oh no... would she lose her hair?

Dr. Brooks let out a chuckle and dropped his pen. "Oh no, nothing like that. Your exam is perfect. Nothing suspicious that raises concerns for a mass. No neuro deficits." She stared at him blankly. He quickly caught on to her confusion. "Meaning: your neurological exam is perfect. If I had a medical student, I'd make them come in here and examine you because you're so... *normal*. Now, that being said—" Dr. Brooks trailed off and tore a piece of paper away from his jotted scribblings. "I *do* want to get an MRI—just as a precaution to ensure we aren't missing anything. Plus, some standard bloodwork. Check your thyroid, vitamin D levels, that sort of stuff."

Mrs. Combs grasped the paper and looked at it glumly. "What you're saying is... something could still be wrong with me?"

Dr. Brooks flapped his hand dismissively. "Nothing in medicine is ever 100% so I can't promise there will be *nothing* wrong but essentially, what we're doing here is dotting our i's and crossing our t's. It'd be a damn shame if I prescribed you migraine medications without fully evaluating you. But if I had to guess? You're developing adult-onset migraines which are very common. Probably triggered by *The Change*. Easy enough to treat. Now go get those tests done so we can start making you feel better!"

That very day, she headed down to the lab and had a purple smocked phlebotomist collect her blood in tubes capped with different colors. The next week she spent several agonizing hours in an MRI machine, listening to horrendous clanks that reminded her of a WW2 submarine movie she'd watched on TV a few weeks ago with her husband, a veritable war nut.

Everything came back normal. Totally fine. But it wasn't. Far from it. She took the meds he prescribed and found they didn't do a damn thing other than lighten her pocketbook. Status migrainosus: that was the diagnosis Dr. Brooks bestowed upon her.

"But not anymore," Mrs. Combs whispered to herself, a grain silo flying past her window.

A paper airplane materialized, sailing into the second row of seats. Giggles followed.

Turning—neck muscles clenching painfully, sending another bolt of fire into her eye—Mrs. Combs yelled, "Hey! Who threw that? Absolutely not. No. Not on my bus."

Ten children met her stern gaze, each having the wherewithal to strive for an innocent expression that only served to make them all appear guilty. She stared at each of them in turn, flicking her eyes back to the road periodically until she felt she'd gotten the point across. She sighed. Sometimes even farm kids were booger snots.

Her days blended back then, marked only by SEVERE HEADACHE and NOT-SO-BAD HEADACHE. Often while driving, the road doubled, tripled, before her very eyes, vision wavering as pain intensified. Sharp lightning struck her temples each time she moved her head or craned her neck to look at her blind spot.

Once, she had to slam on the brakes—leaving skid marks on the road—to avoid plowing into an idling car waiting to make a left-hand turn. The kids had cheered, laughing uproariously when the car's driver laid on the horn and flipped her the bird. Shame filled her. There was no doubt in her mind that some of the kids would casually share over dinner that: Mrs. Combs almost hit a car and then the driver flipped her the bird! Then what? The school board wouldn't be happy—hell, they might even have fired her!

She considered resigning, but her career prospects were limited. Before the school bus, she drove an 18-wheeler, and she *certainly* couldn't take certain medications while driving one of those bemouths. Essentially, her only skills were driving and maintaining a current CDL.

About a week after nearly crushing the car, Mrs. Combs drove an empty school bus back to the barn. Her normal route was closed, marked with orange cones and detour signs. She stuck with less travelled roads when she could—the fewer cars the better; less things to potentially hit when blinding pain took hold. Her hand was forced with the detour though, and she followed its directions. Instead of emerald farms, there were billboards advertising ambulance chaser attorneys, dueling Starbucks and Dunkin' Donuts locations on adjacent corners and—

She remembered seeing it and slamming on the brakes, gaping at the billboard before her, a sign from God, her proverbial burning bush. A beautiful woman in a pristine white coat with a matching flawless smile looked down at her. A stethoscope was casually slung around her neck, but it looked too immaculate, as if it had never been used and was merely a medical prop. And while the woman was stunning—that wasn't what caught her attention.

> **TIRED OF HEADACHES? MEDICATIONS NOT WORKING? LOOK NO FURTHER! CALL DR. ABSINTHE TODAY AND LEARN ABOUT THE DRUG-FREE HEADACHE CURE! JOIN OUR TRIAL NOW!**

A phone number followed which Mrs. Combs hastily typed into her flip phone and saved. Her spirits lifted for the first time in ages. Maybe—just maybe—this Dr. Absinthe was the answer to her prayers!

And she had been.

Today was just a bad day. A fluke. Too little sleep and caffeine coupled with too much noise. It would give anyone—even someone with Dr. Absinthe's chip in place—a headache.

Last stop. The Petersons, a ramshackle shanty held together by hope and scavenged wood. Addie and Jack hopped on—each sporting high-water jeans that would no doubt be picked apart by their cohorts. With a full bus—no children absent today, not on field trip day—Mrs. Combs turned onto Cummings Street, the motor rumbling as she picked up speed. Cummings was lined by businesses: boutiques catering exclusively to rich women with self-esteem issues who had money to burn, CrossFit gyms packed with people that lived and breathed macros and muscle fatigue, and right before the bridge, a small coffee shop packed with mismatched chairs that attracted college students deep in the throes of studying.

More raucous laughter sent a prickle over Mrs. Combs' scalp. Out of her peripheral version, she spied something white streak by.

SMASH!

The rearview mirror shattered to pieces, glass raining down on the dusty floor. Several shards skittered across Mrs. Combs' skin, some spouting teeth and drawing blood. *Those little fucking shits,* she hissed to herself, *ungrateful bastards.* And the prickling of her scalp grew thorns, transforming into something else altogether: pure, all-encompassing wrath.

Her blood pressure rocketed up as epinephrine spilled into her bloodstream, taxing the fragile cerebellar artery residing in her brain since birth. Her vision blurred, making the red sports car in front of the bus appear fuzzy. Blacktop wavered. Instinctually, Mrs. Combs' right foot tapped on the brake. Her red taillights briefly flared—then darkened.

Vision tripled and a bomb exploded at the base of Mrs. Combs' skull. Blurred surroundings turned black as pain overwhelmed the world and—in the skull, adjacent to where the migraine chip resided—an artery burst. Blood filled the nooks and crannies, and more arteries burst in a bizarre domino effect. The sanguine fluid filled each crevice of brain.

Like cement—the blood, chock full of donut-shaped red blood cells—wormed its way into Mrs. Combs' ventricles where clear cerebrospinal fluid circulated. The blood gummed up the ventricles, halting any further movement of CSF. It became a chain reaction and—one by one—the ventricles clogged. Like any brain, hers was very sensitive to such changes and had survival mechanisms built in to combat such insults. Mechanisms that worked briefly, maintaining the delicate cerebral perfusion pressure within its normal parameters.

But every brain had its tipping point—the point of no return, and Mrs. Combs met hers with blinding speed. The brain swelled and herniated downwards, obliterating all brainstem functions that controlled automatic functions like breathing.

Blood poured from Mrs. Combs' ruined arteries like a broken pipe, filling every space with crimson fluid, overwhelming the brain within seconds. Spongy brain matter pushed through the skull's opening—the foreman magnum—enveloping Mrs. Combs' spinal cord in a fatal hug. Teeth clamped around her tongue, filling Mrs. Combs' mouth with coppery blood she didn't taste, and each limb tightened, then spasmed.

Both hands—always at 10 and 2 on her steering wheel—pulled in opposite directions, her dominate hand eventually overwhelming her weaker left, pulling the bus to the right. Right foot slammed down. Had it slammed down on the brake... things might have turned out differently. But it didn't.

Foot stamped down on the gas pedal, surging the bus forward. Directly towards the edge of the bridge. And the brackish river below.

2

Shawn

T HE CANNED BRIGHT LIGHTS seared my pupils and sent a dagger through each juicy eyeball. Squinting helped but only so much. Getting the hell out of H-E-B would be most beneficial; the grocery store was the epitome of sensory overload: kids screaming, cashiers noisily ringing up orders, and competing announcements—*Call for deli on line one... Delivery at the dock*—periodically interrupting the bland Muzak playing in the background.

I brought the list closer to my face and examined Rachel's pointed scrawl. The words blurred; each letter surrounded by a fuzzy halo.

Shit. Not good.

My doc called it a *prodrome*: a fancy medical word for *warning*. "Here, Shawn," he said, handing me a foil packet. "Let's try these. Take one when you start experiencing your prodrome—the halos, the light and sound sensitivity—just pop it under your tongue and wait. Most patients report a near 50% improvement in their headache symptoms and some see complete migraine abortive effects!" He'd looked so pleased with himself, so sure that *this* was the miracle cure. He clearly worshipped at the feet of Big Pharma.

I had reservations about the meds—especially after he casually listed off a list of side effects including but not limited to loose stools, anaphylaxis, increased risk of developing infections, and lethal heart rhythms—but after a shriek echoed from the fruit section, leaving my ears ringing with tinny bells, I knew my choices were limited. Like coach used to say: the definition of insanity was doing the same thing over and over while expecting different results. If I did nothing, I was guaranteed a corker of a migraine—and the thunderstorm roiling between my ears was picking up steam with every passing second.

Might as well nut up and try the damn pill. Even if it turned out to be nothing more than an expensive sugar pill like all the rest. I grabbed my wallet and thumbed through it. Credit cards. Fifty bucks in cash: two twenties and a ratty ten. An old receipt from Whataburger. Shit... did I lose it? Drop it? Or leave it at home? A sour pit churned my stomach and a briny burp shot up my throat, accompanied by hot vomit I swallowed back down—barely. Heart pounding—*please please please be here*—I finally found it in the pouch that used to house condoms when I was on the road. I snatched the foil packet up and despite my shaking fingers, popped a pink pill out. My guts bubbled and my diaphragm clenched.

Here goes nothing, I thought.

Closing my eyes, I placed the teardrop shaped pill under my tongue as instructed. A bitter medicinal taste bloomed, triggering another bout of nausea I barely controlled. Would it kill them to make medicine that didn't taste like absolute shit? I was no stranger to barfing, but it didn't mean I enjoyed it. Who liked tugging half-digested spaghetti noodles out of their nostrils? Do not puke. Do NOT. Spit filled my mouth and my salivary glands throbbed.

"Clean up on Aisle 11," blasted from the intercom. "Clean up on Aisle 11. Customers, use caution in Aisle 11." A high-pitched whine tore through the air at the announcement's end and hot pokers buried themselves deep within my skull, really dug in. The shelves of bread wavered. Blurred. Beads of cold sweat dripped down my back and the world tipped, completely upsetting my equilibrium. Sea sickness on dry land. Vertigo. And I knew what that meant.

I took a staggering step. I had to sit down before—

A curtain of black descended, shuttering my vision, and the tone went out of my legs.

"Hey, you okay?" someone said, their voice coming from the other end of a long tunnel, echoing but somehow diluted.

SMACK!

Down I went, out like a light.

At least unconsciousness offered a brief respite from the pain.

3

Rachel

I TYPED ON THE Pyxis' keypad and the machine emitted a loud beep. "Dammit," I muttered, putting my hands on my hips. Did I spell the medication name wrong or was it just being temperamental like always?

"Hey Rach, isn't that your hubby?" Tamara called out as EMS rolled a patient past the nurses' station.

"My hubby?" I asked, turning my attention from the Pyxis and the hunt for Room 14's Proparacaine. They were already out of view. "What?" I must have misheard. My husband?

Tamara gestured with a thumb. "They took him to 12." She shrugged. "Sure looked like your tall drink of water, anyway. I could be wrong; my eyes are shit these days."

I hurried to Room 12 as they were unloading the patient, working together to go from EMS cot to stretcher, careful not to jostle him excessively since he wore a c-collar to protect a (maybe) broken neck. One look at the patient's face told me all I needed to know:

Tamara's eyes were correct; it *was* my husband.

A sense of déjà vu struck me; reminiscent of when we'd met for the very first time. "Shawn! What the hell happened?" I asked, weaving through medics, nurses, and techs crowding the room until I made it to the head of the bed. "I thought you were going to the store?" A thought occurred to me. "Oh no! You didn't get into a car accident, did you?" A nasty goose egg decorated his forehead. And an MVA would explain the c-collar.

Shawn had a sheepish expression on his face, marred by minute forehead wrinkles that signaled his pain. I'd seen 'em a time a two before. "No, hon, I—"

"—passed out at H-E-B. Went plum out and crashed to the floor. Said he's got himself a wicked headache," one of the medics cut in. Captain Obvious. Then as an afterthought added, "Oh, his blood sugar was 92."

My husband offered up a grimace. "That about sums it up. He left out the part where I puked all over. Waking up in a puddle of your own puke... would not recommend." That would explain his absence of a T-shirt... not that I was complaining about seeing my husband's bare chest, but I would rather it not be in the ER while he was a patient.

I placed my hand on his head, careful to avoid the bump that had to hurt like hell. "I thought you were on new meds? What happened?"

Shawn's lips turned downwards. "What always happens? The migraine took me the fuck out. I popped the pill the second the prodrome started up, but it didn't do shit other than make me feel like puking."

I watched my coworkers flit around the room: placing IVs, drawing blood, and attaching Shawn to the cardiac monitor. "It's okay, we'll get you all checked out and get you something for the pain. We'll make you feel better." Although I didn't feel the least bit happy, I shot him what I hoped passed for a reassuring smile.

Eyes to the ceiling—thanks to the rigid c-collar limiting his movement—Shawn said in a husky voice, "I'm... I'm just so fucking sick of it." Unspent tears brightened his brown eyes. "I can't even go grocery shopping without a migraine ruining everything."

"Hon, it's okay—" I started.

"No. It's not okay," he interrupted. "What would have happened if I was driving when this one hit this bad, Rachel? This could've been worse. Much worse. This one came on me fast... wicked fast. I barely had any warning and..." he trailed off.

I searched my brain for the right answer and unable to find it, I instead grabbed Shawn's hand and squeezed. "I'm here with you, okay, hon? Always."

"Okay," Shawn answered, his voice smaller than his massive frame.

Two CT scans later—head and cervical spine, thankfully negative for any bleeding or fractures—and a heaping helping of IV medications helped. Shawn's migraine went from a 10 to a 7, quite the improvement given he endured a constant 9 to 10 at baseline. I couldn't imagine the agony he lived through daily.

"Ready to go home, hon?" I asked as one of my colleagues pulled his IV and held steady pressure at his antecubital fossa before placing a cotton ball on the pinhole and slapping a Band-Aid over it with practiced efficiency.

Shawn gave a glum nod—finally free of the restrictive collar.

"Come on, let's get you out of here," I said, offering up my arm which Shawn gratefully accepted. The hospital gown stopped mid-thigh on him—it dwarfed most folks but since my hubs was a former NBA player, it looked like an oversized T-shirt. Despite his feeble protests, he had to wear it; he had no other choice. They'd cut his puke-stained shirt off him at H-E-B and I couldn't have him galivanting around the hospital shirtless; they'd mistake him for an escaped psych patient and that was the last thing we needed right now. We slowly walked to the employee parking lot with arms intertwined. I stole a look at Shawn who wore a pensive expression. "You doin' okay?" I asked.

Shawn's mournful brown eyes met mine, looking the part of a sad puppy dog. "I'm just so fucking tired of this, you know? I can't even live a normal life. I thought I might get better once time went on."

I injected my voice with as much positivity as I could muster. "I know, hon. I know. But we can make it through anything together, even this. I'm here for you no matter what. Migraines and all." It wasn't a surprise to me or anything; I knew what I signed up for.

4

Shawn

I VEGGED OUT ON the couch and watched the documentary series *The Last Dance*, all about Michael Jordan's dynasty with the Chicago Bulls. A dull roar filled the space between my ears—like it always did—but today's was a manageable migraine... for now, anyway. Still, a large salad bowl waited on the coffee table in case I upchucked. I popped a ginger candy in my mouth. They were supposed to help with nausea and didn't constipate me like Zofran—I'd become quite the expert on pharmacologics since becoming a professional patient.

My phone buzzed, rattling against the coffee table and I picked it up, mostly to silence the damn noise. I needed to put the sucker on silent.

Lewis Perry flashed across the screen.

Perry? Why was *he* calling? Even though I absolutely didn't want to chat—all I wanted to do was relax on the couch, maybe take a nap—curiosity got the better of me. "Hello?" I said, grabbing the remote and hitting the mute button. On screen, Jordan did one of his characteristic dunks that earned him the moniker of Air Jordan and a flicker of jealousy shot through me. If only I could still do that. If only.

"Shawn! What up my man!" Perry answered, his voice deep and jubilant.

I looked around, taking in my lived-in sweatpants and empty Gatorade bottles strewn about. "Oh, you know... living the dream." Code for: please kill me now.

"Good to hear, good to hear," Perry said, clearly unaware of the true meaning of my words. "Listen man, I was calling to see if you had any interest in joining my basketball team."

I chuckled. "You puttin' together a team of washed up has beens or what, Perry?"

He laughed. "Bro, you ain't a has been, don't dog yourself like that! You got injured. There's a difference. No, it's a charity game for the local children's hospital here. Get ourselves some b-ballers, some reality TV stars, and other celebs, we all play together and charge a fuck ton of money for tickets. Raise money for a good cause and hang out with cool peeps. Supposedly some of those Real Housewives are playing. What do you say?"

On cue, a sharp proverbial knife embedded itself in my right temple and black dots danced in my vision. As much as I'd like to join a charity basketball game, I was in *no* shape to do so. "I fricking wish I could, man," I answered. "Still laid up from the damn injury."

"No shit?" Perry asked. "That was *years* ago."

"No shit," I repeated. "It blows."

"Still having the headaches then?"

Another lance of pain shot through me, this one at the base of my skull. If only he knew about my damn headaches. "Yep," I answered. "Sure am."

"So, get this: Bev suffered from horrible migraines back in the day. Had one almost every other day and she'd tried everything. Pills, injections, she even went to some dude that realigned her chakras... whatever those are. Nothing worked. But then she went to Dr. Absinthe and just like that, no more headaches," Perry said.

I pushed myself into a seated position. "Dr. Absinthe? Isn't that the alcohol they drank on that *EuroTrip* movie, and they hallucinated green fairies and shit? Weird name."

Perry said, "I dunno. I don't watch a lot of the same trash you do, dude. But seriously, this Dr. Absinthe is a miracle worker. Plus, she's hot as hell."

"Okay, I'll bite. What's this Dr. Absinthe's schtick? Does she use leeches or perform lobotomies or what?" I wasn't about to get myself all excited about this so-called miracle cure; I'd heard a million of them and tried most. They always turned out to be snake oil and empty promises.

"Nah, nothing that barbaric or old school. She put this chip in Bev's head—some sort of inhibiting chip or something—and just like that the headaches stopped. She'd had it for a few months and is like a whole new woman," Perry said. "Honest, Shawn, it was a bona fide miracle. We'd tried everything. Saw a whole bunch of docs for it, most of them quacks. It's like she has her whole life back."

Despite myself, despite all the miracle cures that turned out to be a pile of horseshit, hope stirred. "No shit?"

"Absolutely no shit my dude. Listen, I'll send you her details. What do you got to lose?"

He had a point there.

5

D R. ABSINTHE'S RECEPTION AREA and waiting room were decorated with sharp lines and shapes often seen in trendy hotel lobbies. Abstract art—vaguely anatomical in appearance if one squinted and tilted their head to the left—hung against a cool gray. Certainly not the dour decorations seen in most neurology offices: mismatched end tables whose drawers were filled with dust bunnies and crumbled ancient Rolaids, topped with magazines years out of date; illustrations of the central and peripheral nervous systems adorning otherwise bare walls; puffy pink stress balls shaped like brains in baskets, harbingers of flu rather than relaxation. Billie ought to know—she spent her teen years consulting with migraine specialists in far flung locales.

Billie swiped a magazine on her way to the breakroom. Magazines: one major perk of her receptionist gig; the employer matched 401k a close second. Dr. Absinthe subscribed to *Glamour, US Weekly,* and *Sports Illustrated* or as she'd said once: The Holy Trinity. No boring medical journals. The week Billie started work she asked Dr. Absinthe why she didn't just toss medical journals on the tables like all other neurologists did.

Dr. Absinthe joked to Billie: "You have a few neurologists in the family? You know *all* about their dry reading material."

Billie replied, "No neurologists. We've got a podiatrist that loves talking about diabetic foot wounds at Thanksgiving Dinner though. Mom hates it but he still gets invited each year. No... I've seen a few neurologists myself. As a patient." Billie pointed to her temple. "Migraines."

"Migraines?" Dr. Absinthe asked. "Really?"

"Had 'em real bad when I was a teenager. Puberty and all that," Billie said. "All the hormones wreaked havoc on my body. Becoming a woman really sucked honestly."

Dr. Absinthe nodded, a thoughtful look on her face. "If you don't mind me asking: do you still get them?"

Billie reflexively went to lie, to say: *no, it's all good*—even though it wasn't good at all and surprised herself and told the truth. "I mean... yeah. They're not as bad as they were but..." she trailed off.

"Still not great then?" Dr. Absinthe asked.

"Right," Billie agreed.

Dr. Absinthe picked up a gossip magazine and looked at the cover. "Patients don't want to read boring medical crap. Too depressing. Let them read *Real Housewife Behind Bars* if it makes them forget they have ALS for a few minutes," Dr. Absinthe said, answering Billie's earlier question. "Don't you think?"

Billie voiced her agreement. A doctor's office was already enough of a bummer with all the terminal illnesses, chronic diseases, and whatnot. Plus, it was much better reading material.

"And just so you know: migraines are kind of my thing." Dr. Absinthe grinned and readjusted her glasses. "I've been working on a treatment that's almost ready for prime time."

"Really?" Billie asked.

And like they said: the rest was history. Not only was Billie Dr. Absinthe's receptionist—she was also Dr. Absinthe's patient.

Billie flopped down in what she considered *her chair* in the breakroom and turned her attention to the magazine, intermittently cackling as she thumbed through the back issue of *Glamour*. The coffee machine burbled in the corner and the mint green refrigerator hummed. "Now ain't this some shit," Billie remarked.

Pages fluttered.

"What?" Claire said around a mouthful of blueberry muffin. She wiped crumbs off her surgical green scrub top, knocking her RN badge off in the process. It landed with a clatter and skidded under the table. "Shit," she remarked and stared forlornly at the floor.

"I'm reading this magazine." Billie shook the pages for theatrical effect. "And an article about blowjobs pops up," Billie said, grinning at her pun. Her eyebrows waggled with good humor.

Claire groaned, rolling her eyes as she fumbled for her badge. "Blowjobs, right. You were saying?"

Billie pulled a serious face. "I mean... do you think I should tear that article out? Don't I have some sort of civic responsibility or something?"

Straightening—still badge-less—Claire frowned. "What? Why? You wanna tape it to your bathroom mirror? Learn how to give good head while brushing your teeth? Or because you want to protect our patients from a healthy sex life?"

Billie flapped her hand. "No. I can't give head—you know that. Because of my *condition*." Billie pointed at her jaw. "I've got TMJ." Her face broke into a wicked grin. "At least, that's what I tell Jerry. *Such a tragedy, sure wish I could, hon.*" Her voice lilted up in a Southern drawl.

"Then why do you want to tear it out?" Claire asked.

"Claire, do you really think it's smart to have an article about blowjobs where some epileptic housewife can read it and decide she wants to spice up her sex life? What if she has a seizure while giving a BJ?" Billie snapped her jaws and enamel clinked together. "It's like a dick guillotine."

Claire laughed. "That's gross, Billie but... *Dick Guillotine* would make a great band name. And I understand your concern when you put it that way. Tear it out."

Soft bells cued, eliciting twin groans.

"This commercial is going to drive me fucking crazy one day," Billie said. She closed her eyes and rubbed her temples in slow circles. "The irony honestly."

"Of what?" Claire said.

Billie answered, "I get this chip that completely stopped all my migraines *except* for the headaches caused by the commercial *for* the migraine chip. A real Catch-22."

Claire gave the receptionist a sympathetic look. Given that there was a huge flat screen TV mounted next to the receptionist counter, poor Billie was practically waterboarded with the commercial. She routinely complained to Dr. Absinthe—and anyone within earshot—that it had to be a human rights violation of some kind to continuously stream it. "I'll call Alanis Morrisette so she can update her song in honor of your plight," Claire remarked.

"Who?" Billie's eyebrows arched up comically.

Claire groaned. "What? You Gen Z'ers don't know Alanis? *Ironic*? Great song."

"Nope." Billie said.

"Ugh." The soft bells cued again. "I bet those cute little bells make you feel like Pavlov's dog," Claire said.

"Seriously," Billie replied. "One day I'll probably be out in public and hear them and it'll activate some sleeper agent setting. Eliminate some high-powered target with secret Kungfu. Or lose my mind. One or the other." Billie shrugged, *what can you do?*

Other doctors' offices played Fox News; the high-powered specialties like plastics or dermatology who abhorred high taxes, or The Weather Channel; comprised of doctors addicted to golf and sunny days or ER folks who could count on lots of hip fractures when it iced over. Not Dr. Absinthe's office. All TVs played her ad continuously, ever since its debut the year prior.

"Yeah, that's enoughof that," Billie said, inclining her head to the screen. She tossed the magazine on the table and popped in her headphones. Claire quickly followed suit.

In the waiting room, an elderly gentleman filled out paperwork. His pen skittered across the forms with the shaky scrawl of Parkinson's disease; his thin shoulders hunched forward, giving him a frail, stooped appearance. Hearing the advertisement's tones, he hastily jotted down the last of his information and set the pen and clipboard in his lap—ready to pay rapt attention to the screen. He rather enjoyed Dr. Absinthe's well-tailored white coat and low-cut blouse revealing the perfect hint of cleavage.

A lush garden materialized onscreen, speckled with multi-colored flowers bobbing in a light breeze. From the right of the screen Dr. Absinthe strode into frame and shot the camera a blindingly white grin. "Hi there. I'm Dr. Aldea Absinthe, board-certified neurologist. Are you tired of living with pounding headaches day after day? Sick of debilitating migraines that leave you unable to live the life you want? The life you deserve?"

She pointed to her temple.

"Then look no further! No more forcing down bitter pills. No nasty injections, hoping for—at best—mild to moderate relief." She flashed her megawatt grin, showing off perfectly straight teeth. "I can offer you TOTAL relief from your headaches."

The screen rippled and changed.

A frowning, frumpy woman sat on an exam table, dressed in a thin blue gown. Ragged fingernails dug into her temples as she massaged in small circles. Eeyore personified.

Knock knock.

Dr. Absinthe burst into the exam room, white coat fluttering behind her.

The elderly man suppressed a grin, eyes homed in on Dr. Absinthe's breasts. His trouser mouse twitched; something it hadn't done in a long time. Dr. Absinthe truly was a miracle worker.

Onscreen, Dr. Absinthe continued: "With my new inhibiting chip, you too can live a migraine free life! Imagine going through your day without fear of a horrific headache ruining everything. No more missed dance recitals, cancelled dates. You can *live*."

The woman stopped rubbing her head and stared at Dr. Absinthe, mouth agape. "You mean, I can go back to my old life?" she asked, voice filled with wonder.

Dr. Absinthe tipped the audience a wink; the mascara liberally applied to her long eyelashes made her soft brown color pop against the baby blue wallpaper. "You sure can! My patented inhibiting chip implanted at the base of your skull acts immediately to block neurons responsible for your misery. And my success rate speaks for itself. Patients report a more than 75% decrease in their pain with nearly all achieving complete relief a few months after chip implantation."

The screen cut from Dr. Absinthe's face to a rendered image of a brain, red starbursts blooming over its surface. A non-descript gray chip flew into view, blue waves radiating outwards. Blue overpowered angry red. A wicked thunderclap sound effect gave way to more soothing chimes.

Former dumpy woman with wrecked cuticles made another appearance except her face no longer bore the pinched expression of the supremely constipated and her mousy brown hair shone with luster. Years had dropped away. The woman proclaimed, "Thanks to Dr. Absinthe, I can return to my old life, pain-free!"

Swooping text filled the screen and a baritone voice rattled off:

"Call now, 555-0420 for your free consultation. Don't let headaches hold you back! Leave your brain in Dr. Absinthe's capable hands and start living your life again!" Then like an auctioneer: "ChipsnotFDAapproved."

The commercial faded to black. A minute passed. The bells chimed and the commercial replayed. And would continue to do so until quitting time.

Not that the elderly gentleman objected one bit.

6

Shawn

I SAT IN EXAM Room 3, lamenting the freezing metal beneath my bony ass. Why did I have to wear this stupid gown anyway? Last I checked I was here for headaches not a prostate exam. But I'd smiled at the nurse—Claire per the badge—and did as I was told, shucking my shirt and sweats. I kept my Garfield and Odie boxer shorts and black athletic socks on. Both offered meager protection from the artic ambient temperature. My left leg jittered, as it did when I was overcome with boredom or nerves. The table rattled; I looked up. The wall clock's minute hand ticked past three. Fifteen minutes late—classic doctor move.

Inside my skull, dull ache sharpened until a pointed ice pick stabbed through each eyeball. A thin hiss escaped my lips, and I squeezed my eyes shut. Electric slivers shot through my face into each tooth, like chewing on tin foil with a mouthful of dental fillings. Each root throbbed. Shocked at how I *never* got used to the pain, even after all these years—I sent up a prayer: *Please, please, please don't let Dr. Absinthe be some quack.* Although... truth be told I didn't really believe in God. How could I? The bastard snatched away my charmed life, doused it in gasoline and struck a match. Torched it straight to the ground.

Knock, knock!

"It's Dr. Absinthe. Can I come in?"

The roar between my ears ebbed but my heart rate spiked. "Um... yeah, come in!" I called, voice cracking at *yeah* like a teenager in the throes of puberty. I inwardly cringed.

The door swung inward, and Dr. Absinthe walked in, immediately offering me her right hand. "Hi there. I'm Dr. Absinthe. Nice to meet you!" Grasping her hand in mine, I gave it the firm shake my agent taught me long ago. Her palm felt warm and impossibly soft; lots of lotion probably.

"Shawn Gilbert," I said. No embarrassing crack this time. I breathed a sigh of relief.

Delicately, she sat on a silver stool, turned—facing me—and gave me a wry smile. "Shawn Gilbert. I never thought I'd meet you, let alone have you as a patient! I loved watching you as a kid." Chocolate brown eyes glittered; the same color as Rachel's.

Heat bloomed on my cheeks and my ears followed suit—like always. Even in the height of Gilbert Fever, I got embarrassed. But post-retirement? I felt so awkward about it. I rubbed the back of my neck and tense knots meet my fingertips. "Uh... thanks."

Her eyes cut conspiratorially to the door. "My nurse, Claire, made fun of me, but I brought a basketball in. I was hoping—" She stopped and giggled girlishly. "—maybe you'd sign it?"

How long had it been since someone asked me to autograph something?

Flashes streaked through my mind, pulling me back into a quagmire of memories.

Pulling up in the team bus; walking to the arena dressed in one of my sharp suits—tailored, of course—a pair of Gilberts on my feet. The crowds. So many people. Most wore jerseys—usually mine although my teammates Baylon and Rev were popular runners-up—and on spotting me, they screamed my name. Chanted. Those hugging the barrier thrust things into my path: posters, glossy headshots, and T-shirts. Very cliché but I'd had a few pairs of panties tossed my way.

Such a long time ago. I blinked and the exam room came back into sharp focus. Dr. Absinthe clutched the basketball—seemingly pulled from nowhere—with a hopeful expression. "Of course; I'll sign it. Does that mean I get a discount on my bill?" I quipped.

She winked. "I'll see what I can do on my end. Here," she said, tossing the ball to me. Automatically my hands rose to meet it. The familiar slap of bumpy rubber against my palms sent a pang of sadness through me. "Let me grab you a Sharpie," she said. Turning her attention to her white coat, she rummaged through the pockets.

I cleared my throat. "So... did you play basketball?" I asked.

She laughed. "I tried. Me on defense? MVP. Great. Offense? Terrible. I often forgot to dribble the ball which—as you can imagine—is a big impediment." Returning her attention to Operation Sharpie, she added, "I'm more of a sport-without-a-ball kind of gal. But I loved watching it. Still do."

"Dribbling can be tricky, to be fair," I said.

"A-ha! Found it." She tossed me the black marker. Uncapping it, I scrawled my signature—nostalgia hanging heavily over me. "Thanks again for signing that. I wish I could go back in time and tell younger me this would happen." Her dainty fingers flashed over the keyboard, and she peered at the computer monitor, shifting into doctor mode. "So, you're experiencing migraines, then? Tell me more about that," she said, leaning forward.

A bolt of lightning went off in my head and I winced. "Well... to tell the truth, I've got one right now."

Dr. Absinthe's eyebrows knitted with concern. "Can I get you something for that?" She gestured towards the exam room door. "I can have Claire give you an injection or..."

I waved my hand. "Nah, it's okay. I'm used to it. Plus... nothing helps anyway." It really didn't. I'd tried damn near everything. Tylenol, Motrin, Excedrin, Magnesium, Riboflavin, medications with unpronounceable names.

Baylon recommended rubbing molasses clockwise on the temples. Saw him do it a few times in the locker room before a game when he was hungover. Didn't do a damn thing for me other than make me sticky.

Soak your feet in a hot bath to draw out the migraine? Felt nice; did zip.

I saw tons of neurologists, each putting me through tests like a lab rat. Loud clanging MRIs. EEGs. Vials of blood sent to far away labs—draining me like medical vampires.

As much as I hated to admit it, I even tried the various "cures" found in the back pages of *The National Enquirer*. You know the type: **Tired of being fat? For only 4 payments of $29.99, you can buy the best fat-burner!** I ordered an amulet promising to chase away demons responsible for headaches. **Made by a Native American Medicine Man** or so the ad claimed. One quick glimpse of the bottom revealed a **Made in China** stamp.

Another ad touted healing crystals purported to draw bad energy out. I remembered seeing them in downtown shops near the *Keep Austin Weird* t-shirts. I purchased three—Amethyst, Agate, a Clear Quartz—with high hopes that *this* would be the answer. Nope. They resided on the living room mantle next to our wedding photos; pretty, but useless.

Botox, acupuncture, mushroom tea that tasted like dog shit seasoned with a hint of acorns, I'd run through the gamut. The only thing that came close to helping was weed which took the headache from 10 to 9.7. More so it made everything hilarious. I spent hours parked in front of the TV with a bowl of popcorn laughing until I wheezed.

I'd scoured the ends of the Earth, searching for mythical roots. This. That. Always destined for disappointment when touted miracle cure turned became just another dud. I'd tried it all and then some.

Dr. Absinthe was my last hope.

I sighed. "I'm sure you saw the headlines and watched the highlight reels. One wrong move and my career? Over. Like that." I snapped my fingers. "Afterwards, dribbling a ball—just dribbling—left my head ringing." I shrugged and added, "The resultant depression sort of sucked too, not gonna lie."

Dr. Absinthe gave me a smile. "On the bright side: I—" She solemnly placed a hand on her chest. "—would have never developed a migraine from dribbling."

I chuckled. "That's true."

"I'm sorry for all the suffering you've endured. Life's really not fair." She stared down at her hands. "Like my mom used to say: *life's a bitch and then you die.* You got dealt a bad hand, that's for sure."

"Yup," I replied. No arguments there.

She tapped her fingers against her thighs. "Without you, well, the team—they uh—"

"—sucked?" I finished for her.

Dr. Absinthe thrust her hands up. "Hey, you said it, not me!"

"Doctor-patient confidentiality remember? This is a safe space. Or so you said." I joked.

"That's true." She picked up a pen and pointed at me with a wink. "So, I reviewed your questionnaire, and it looks like you've tried everything short of an exorcism." I snorted and she raised an eyebrow. "Sounds ridiculous but I've had patients try it. Not that it worked. At least, not for their headaches. Helped with inner demons though from what I hear," Dr. Absinthe said with a grin.

"Yeah, didn't try that one. Not yet anyway." Had I thought of it, I probably would have.

She shook her head. "I don't think you're going to have to resort to that. Here's the thing, Mr. Gilbert—"

"Shawn," I cut in. "Call me Shawn."

"Shawn," she repeated. "After reviewing your most recent labs and imaging, I think you would be an ideal candidate for my migraine chip. Your blood pressure is great. You don't smoke. And you've—quite honestly—exhausted every option short of a lobotomy: something I also do not recommend for the record. I think you could benefit from this." She paused. "But—"

But? Nothing good ever ended with *but*.

She put her index finger in the air. "But—I gotta caution you. My chips aren't FDA-approved yet. Strictly experimental at this point. Not to say they don't work—they work beautifully—but I haven't jumped through all the hoops yet. Any patient receiving the chip must enroll in my clinical trial. I'll want to run tests too." I must have made a face because she waved a hand. "Nothing too crazy: functional MRIs, blood work, questionnaires, that sort of thing."

"That's fine. I can do that," I said. Sounded reasonable to me. If Dr. Absinthe told me eating a fresh dog turd cured headaches, I would probably try it.

Dr. Absinthe nodded. "One stipulation: for the next six months, you'll need to relocate here. If any untoward complications were to arise, I'd like you nearby so I can manage them appropriately. Personally. Texas is a little too far away I'm sad to say." She raised her hand. "Not that I expect anything to happen, mind you. The chips have proven extremely safe thus far. Just a precaution." She looked at me. "Is that something you can do?"

"I mean... I need to chat with the wife first but yeah. Count me in. Tentatively."

"Of course, discuss it with your wife. The best marriages are based on communication, right? Not that I'd know—I'm not married." Her smile faltered. "If you don't mind me asking; what does she do?"

"She's an ER nurse. We met right after my accident; she took care of me in the ER."

"Okay, that's adorable," Dr. Absinthe remarked. "I'm a romantic at heart so I love a good meet cute like that. If it helps, I can put you in touch with realtors and I know a lot of folks. Easy to put in a good word. The ER is always looking for experienced nurses." Dr. Absinthe stood and shook my hand again. "Talk it over with her and let me know what you think. I think this could be good for you, Shawn."

A thin sprig of something warm sprung up in my chest, a feeling I hadn't felt in some time: Hope.

"I will. Thanks for everything, Dr. Absinthe. I'll be in touch."

She gave me another wink and gestured to the basketball with her thumb. "Thanks again for the autograph!"

She left the exam room and I exhaled shakily, cautioning myself not to get my hopes up.

Not that it helped.

7

Shawn

WITH LACK OF ANYTHING else better to do, I headed back to the airport. The security line was minimal, and I breezed right through. No one recognized me—not even the bored TSA agent who checked my driver's license. I couldn't decide what felt worse; being seen or being invisible. Being anonymous did have its comforts; I had to admit. No one looked at you too closely or judged. The last time I was a no name? Middle school. That's when I got noticed. Some folks were math whizzes; able to manipulate numbers in their head like a computer. Others picked up a paintbrush just *knowing*, like it was an instinct.

I was born for basketball. And I've got my 'rents to thank for that.

Genetics; the ultimate lottery.

Ma grew up in North Carolina, practically born with a basketball in her hands. She had built-in teammates and opponents; her two older brothers. She'd shoot hoops for hours on end in the driveway. Pick-up games with neighborhood kids who played dirty, throwing elbows and busting noses. Made varsity as a freshman; point guard no less. Scored 40 points with 20 assists in the State Final game. Scouts from Duke and the University of North Carolina attended her games—a thrill for any native North Carolinian—along with countless scouts from other programs. Four State Championships. Signed with Duke where she boasted three Final Four appearances and two Championships. Olympic Gold Medal: no big deal, leading the female Dream Team.

That's where she met my Pops. Like *Love & Basketball* except Pops was a track star, not a ball player.

My Pops boasted State and National titles in high school. Signed with the Longhorns, netting a handful of NCAA titles. If you watched a Summer Olympics in the past twenty years, he was there: winning gold—lots of 'em. The 100 and 200m and he usually anchored relays. Moved up to 400m distance and broke records. His last Olympics before retirement? Gold in 100m, 200m, 4x200m relay, and he anchored the 4x400m relay with a 43.7 split.

Basketball was my identity growing up. I lived it. Breathed it. *Loved* it, like you would love a close family member or a treasured family pet. Basketball was my stage.

And now-a-days; no one saw me.

Bummer. But what can you do?

My stomach rumbled at the French fry scent lingering in the air—oil and salt. A combination of nerves and migraine accompanied by nausea meant breakfast was a paltry three Saltine crackers and a Ginger Ale. With my headache at a mere dull roar, I was starving.

McDonald's. Maybe.

Smoothie place: no.

Chili's was out since their head chef was a microwave.

Ditto to the vegan sandwich shop where everything looked like mushy baby shit slathered on gluten-free bread.

I settled on a sports bar boasting sandwiches named for athletes. Much to my chagrin I didn't spot a Gilbert. The waitress popped by as I examined the menu. "What can I get you, hon?" she drawled, punctuating the question with a fierce gum snap.

"How about the All Day IPA and the Jordan? With fries, please," I said.

Acrylic nails clicked against a handheld screen. "Happy Hour is from 2-to-4, half price wings. I recommend buffalo sauce and we got homemade ranch." She waved a hand to her ample waistline. "I could drink the stuff."

I thought of the fat layer on my stomach and cringed. "Better not. No thanks."

"Kay." Another gum snap and she was gone.

My eyes roved over the opposite wall, and I counted the flatscreens. Nine. The biggest had ESPN playing some Talking Head show. Back in the day, I'd been a hot topic of discussion; not so much anymore. A rugby game. Then there was soccer or as the Spanish called it: *fútbol*. A player hurled himself to the ground after minor contact, giving an Oscar-worthy performance.

The waitress swung back by and deposited a sweating pint glass on a coaster. Amber sloshed over glass and hops filled the air. "Thanks!" I called out and took a sip. Savoring the crisp carbonation, I turned my attention back to the wall of TVs.

My stomach dropped.

No way.

It was... *me*.

A floodgate of memories unleashed; things I hadn't felt in a long time.

And like it was yesterday, I was there:

Smell. That's what I remembered most. The rubber scent left on my fingers and palm from the ball. Sweat; my own but everyone else's too. You'd think inhaling other people's B.O. and exertions would be off-putting but I kind of liked it. There was something *pure* about it: the scent of people playing their hearts out. Buttered popcorn—a waft every now and then. Hotdogs and the sugary reek of cotton candy hocked by roving attendants combing the stands. The cheerleaders' perfume: a smorgasbord—floral scents, pine, and a zesty soap scent.

The sounds. The sharp cut of sneakers on freshly buffed gymnasium floor serving as the game's bass rhythm. Meaty thunks when ball hit outstretched hands. Dribbling. Banter with my teammates. Shit-talking with the opposing team or mouthy fans. The roar of the crowd. Their cheers, jeers, and boos always filled me with raw emotion.

I watched myself onscreen, remembering how I'd felt during that game. *Invincible.*

The seconds flickered downwards, noted by both clock and crowd.

"Ten! Nine! Eight!"

We were down by two. The other team had possession and their point guard stormed the key. Sudden surety filled me, and the world slowed. Charging forward as if guided by an unseen hand—I reached out, tipping the ball away mid-dribble. Mine now.

The announcer screamed, barely able to contain his excitement: "LOOK AT GILBERT GO!" The crowd echoed his sentiment, screaming my name. Buoyed by their adoration, I surged forward, repeating in my head: *down by two, down by two.*

"Six!"

The arena rumbled under my feet as I passed half-court. I saw blurs of yellow on either side of me—the opposing team, far too slow to challenge me. The sidelines rippled—a breathing organism—riveted on the unfolding action.

"FIVE!"

Sensing someone nearing me, I crossed the ball behind me, and it sprang into my right palm, and the defender steaked past me—empty handed. Sucker.

"FOUR!"

The three-point line; only steps away. *Down by two. Down by two.*

"THREE!"

Legs rattled seats and my dental fillings vibrated. I pulled up, a foot away from the line.

"TWO!"

Every part of my body—joints, muscles, tendons, neurons—fired in perfect sequence. The ball left my hands.

And I knew.

"ONE!"

The ball soared through the net with a literal swish. Supreme peace filled me.

"Gilbert's done it! THREEEEEEEE!" the announcer called; voice dizzy with jubilation. The buzzer echoed, barely audible over the screaming crowd.

I'd clinched my first NCAA title.

Remembering the day, one of the best days of my life, I choked back tears and realized my fingers were clenched painfully around my glass. I relaxed them, fighting the adrenaline coursing through me, and I realized my other hand was shaking. It made me think of acid flashbacks, episodes—sometimes years later—where you tripped balls again, reexperiencing that high. The euphoria. I'd never personally experienced one myself—despite my fair share of partying—but this had to be what it was like. That clip acted as a personal LSD flashback, taking me right back. They'd set the volume low, so I read the closed captioning unfurling at the bottom of the screen: **And for our #1 buzzer beater moment... Shawn Gilbert clinching the first NCAA title EVER for...**

"Here's the Jordan with fries," the waitress drawled, jolting me out of my reverie. "Ketchup and napkins there," she said, pointing. "And we got hot sauces if you want 'em. Getcha anything else, hon?"

My old life back? I thought but I said, "I'm good, thanks."

While the burger was tasty, it sat like a lead brick in my gut. My stomach churned as I boarded the plane but thankfully, the second I stretched out in first class—I was too tall to sit comfortably in coach—it was lights out. When wheels touched down in Austin, I woke and grimaced. Another headache. I collected the Audi from the parking garage and started the drive home.

"Siri, call Rachel," I said, turning my music down.

The phone rang, rang, rang. I was about to hang up—catching her at work was a longshot—when Rachel answered, sounding out of breath: "Hey babe. What's up?"

A blood-curdling scream echoed in the background.

"Um… everything okay over there?" I asked. Rachel's workdays were never dull. I merged right; my exit was next.

Rachel laughed. "Oh yeah. That's just a full-grown man covered in tattoos terrified to get a tetanus shot." She raised her voice. "Course, the way he's carrying on might make you think his leg was ripped off."

A faint *hey* sounded, in protest.

I chuckled. "Listen, want me to grab anything for dinner? I should be home in thirty or so."

"I won't turn down In-N-Out if you're offering. Cheeseburger and fries, animal style," she said. "But you probably already knew that."

Her old standard. "I know babe, but the one time I don't ask, you'll say you wanted Whataburger instead."

An alarm blared on Rachel's end, and she groaned. "Ugh, Jesus Christ. Gotta go. Code Blue. Love you!"

The call disconnected.

Duty called.

8

Rachel

I CLOCKED OUT THIRTY minutes late—not terrible considering most days were an absolute dumpster fire and I sometimes stayed hours I was supposed to be off. My stomach groaned. Graham crackers smeared with peanut butter didn't qualify as lunch and I'd gobbled those hours ago during my one pee break of the shift. Life as a nurse was great, so glamorous. Pulling on the freeway, I fantasized about burgers slathered with In-N-Out's spread aka nectar of The Gods. My breath would reek of onions—but Shawn wouldn't care; he'd still kiss me. I sighed. Even after nearly ten years, I adored him. Easy on the eyes too—always a plus. It wasn't love at first sight though. More like:

Oh shit, this guy doesn't look so good.

"Brought you a live one," the medic said, rolling the stretcher into the room.

Eyeing the patient, I replied, "I see that." My internal nursing alarm bells weren't quite blaring, but I was on high alert. "He looks like shit," I said under my breath, directing my comment to the medic. Vomit stained the front of the guy's jersey and blood—dried and fresh—adorned his head and he looked gray. Never a great sign. Carefully, we transferred him to the ER stretcher—making damn sure to keep his neck immobilized.

They'd slapped a c-collar on at the scene but as an extra precaution, I placed each gloved palm on either side of his head. He gazed up at me with glassy eyes. Other nurses descended: trauma sheers cut through jersey and shorts and two IVs were placed.

The charge nurse called out, "Yo, what's his name and date of birth? I need to arrive him in the computer."

"Shawn Gilbert, 03/20/80."

Keys clacked as she typed the information in.

Nick's head shot up and he whirled around. "Holy shit, no way!"

"What?" I asked.

Nick shot me an incredulous look. "You're telling me you don't recognize him?"

I glanced at the patient and squinted. "No... should I?"

Nick rolled his eyes. "Uh, yeah! He's only one of the coolest sports stars around."

"Basketball, right?" I asked, remembering the shorts and jersey.

"Yes!" He shook his head and muttered, "I can't work in these conditions. My co-workers don't even know who Shawn Gilbert is, Jesus Christ. So uncultured."

I looked at the patient—Shawn Gilbert: famous basketball star, apparently—and studied him closely. He *was* tall; his lower legs hung off the end of the stretcher but not gargantuan or anything. "What happened?" I asked the medic.

Clutching a clipboard, the medic gave report:

"Shawn Gilbert with no significant past medical history, no allergies, suffered a head injury playing basketball tonight. Got nailed by another player. Positive LOC and he was out for about five minutes. When he came to, he puked but is maintaining his airway... for now. Blood sugar was 120."

Nick called out, "Heart rate is dropping and his pressure... oh shit."

"What?" I asked.

He met my eyes and grimaced. "210/100."

Not good. I ran and grabbed the doctor from another room. "Listen, I need you in Room 1. I think he's got a bleed. Bradycardic and hypertensive as hell." I paused. "And apparently, he's some bigshot NBA player or something. No pressure."

The doc swore—predictably since brain bleeds could go to shit in a hurry—and hustled after me, bemoaning his terrible luck, "Why does this have to go down on my shift? If something happens to him... we'll be on every news channel getting torn apart. Why has God forsaken me yet again?"

"Oh stop feeling sorry for yourself," I replied. "You're not the one with a brain bleed."

Minutes later, I found myself accompanying Shawn Gilbert to CT, pushing his stretcher down the long hallway. The cardiac monitor beeped, displaying Shawn's vitals.

"Ma'am? Ma'am, right? I can't exactly see with this... thing." Shawn reached up and grabbed his c-collar. I opened my mouth, ready to tell him to leave it alone, but he dropped his hand." Am I okay?" he asked, fear saturating each word.

For now, I thought. "Yeah, you're going to be fine," I said, hoping I wasn't lying through my teeth. "Trust me."

"Okay," Shawn replied, staring up at the ceiling. "What happened to me?"

"You don't remember?" I asked.

He seesawed his hand in the air. "I mean... I remember getting my bell rung and then it was lights out. That's about it."

"That sounds like the gist of what happened," I replied. I took a corner too sharply and smacked into the wall, narrowly avoiding smashing Shawn's leg. "Oops. Sorry!"

"Damn! Where'd you learn to drive?"

Straightening the stretcher, I forged on. "In my defense, these are hard to push and you're... big."

"Big? Like fat? You're calling me fat?"

Shit. "I mean—" I started but his laugh interrupted me.

"Just fuckin' with you." he said with unabashed glee. "Ma'am," he added respectfully as an afterthought.

We reached the double doors of CT, and I pressed the automatic button on the wall. "Not ma'am. *Rachel*. 'Ma'am' makes me feel geriatric."

"Nice to meet you, *Rachel*," he replied. His face broke out in a wild grin and my stomach flipped. "I'm Shawn Gilbert." Up his arm went and his hand curled in a fist. "We can't exactly shake on it," he said sheepishly. "Fist bump?"

I tapped his fist. "Fist bumps spread less germs anyway."

"Said like a true germophobic nurse."

Pulling the stretcher up to the CT table, I dropped the railing. "Don't you dare try to move yourself," I admonished. Catching the CT tech's eyes through the glass, I waved her over. Her cohort followed.

"I would never," Shawn said.

Turning to the techs, I said, "Listen, I'll hold c-spine and you guys pull him on the table; on three." They nodded and gripped Shawn's sheet. "Shawn, give yourself a hug," I directed, grasping the sides of Shawn's head—careful of my hand placement, mindful he might have a skull fracture. I looked down, making sure he'd followed my directions. Chocolate brown eyes met mine and he tipped me a wink. *What a flirt*, I thought, suppressing a grin. "One, two, three."

Working in tandem, we slid him over. Shawn remarked, "Smoothest flight I've been on."

"We aim to please," I replied.

"Do you now?" he asked flirtatiously. I had to give him points; the man probably had a devastating brain injury, but he still made time to hit on the ladies.

Ignoring *that*, I pointed at him and said, "Your job? Stay still. Don't wiggle around. Last thing we need is the radiologist acting like a little bitch, whining *it's non-diagnostic*."

"For you? I'll be a statue."

He better. "Good." I angled the cardiac monitor so I could see it from the adjacent room and said, "Let me know if you aren't feeling well, okay?"

He shot me a thumbs up.

I joined the techs at their station, eyes darting between Shawn's cardiac monitor and their computer screen—where his scans would pop up in real time.

"Is that really Shawn Gilbert? The basketball player?" the male tech asked with a wonderstruck expression.

I nodded. "Yup."

"Cool. Do you think he'll sign an autograph for me?"

I said, "How about you do your job, and we'll cross that bridge when we come to it, hmm?"

The other tech pushed some buttons and in the other room, the table descended into the tube. "CT head and cervical spine, right?" she asked; all business.

"Yup," I repeated.

A worm of unease gnawed at me. Shawn's heart rate hovered around forty—nothing too concerning for a healthy, athletic male but it could signal impending brain herniation in the setting of a traumatic head injury. The machine whirred—the sound muffled by the radiation shielding wall—and images populated the screen. "Oh shit," I said, my eyes widening. I hurried to the wall and picked up the phone, dialing the ER doc's extension. "Hey, Shawn Gilbert has a massive epidural. Midline shift. Call neurosurgery. NOW."

High pitched beeping caught my attention, and I whipped my head around and peered at Shawn's monitor. Now his heart rate hovered in the twenties and despite the hydralazine I'd pushed prior to CT, his blood pressure had shot up.

"Rachel? I don't feel so good—" Shawn's tinny voice echoed over the intercom.

"Shit, he's herniating!" I yelled into the receiver, quickly hanging up. Neurosurgery needed called like yesterday. "Stop the scan," I commanded. Without waiting, I rushed into the CT room. "Shawn, what's wrong?" I asked.

Sweat dotted his brow and his eyelids drooped. Checking his eyes sent a chill down my spine. Under the bright lights, it was easy to see his pupils didn't match, further confirming my fears—one normal sized while the other pupil had nearly overtaken the brown of his iris. "I feel sick—I feee—" he slurred. As if recognizing me, his gaze sharpened. "Rachel, don't let me—die."

Oh shit. "I won't," I said to him. Turning, I yelled, "Help me move him! Now!" The techs ran out. "On three!" I grasped his head. "One, two, three!"

The second his body hit the ER cot, he seized. The next thirty minutes passed in a blur of activity. Intubation. More meds and drips than I could count; and then hauling ass to the OR. After delivering him to the scrub nurses, I returned to the ER and rejoined the fray, but Shawn wasn't far from my mind. I thought of the scared look in his eyes, right before he lost consciousness.

Would my face be the last one he ever saw?

I drove home in silence that night, replaying our interaction over and over. He'd made me feel... *something.* I thought of his easy smile, his flirting, his charm. I tossed and turned all night, unable to stop my racing brain. And when I woke:

I worried about Shawn.

And all these years later, I still worried but for other reasons.

I pulled up to the house and parked in the garage. Grabbing my bag and massive water jug, I ambled inside. "Honey, I'm home!" I called out, tossing my keys on the hall table.

Shawn's voice echoed from the living room, "In here, hon!"

I stripped my scrubs off and tossed them directly in the washer. Once you went out in public wearing another person's shit stain, you learned to shuck work clothing immediately. Clad in only a sports bra and undies, I sauntered into the living room. Our massive flat screen TV was on, switched to a basketball game—sound off, subtitles on. Hearing my footsteps, Shawn turned, and a look flickered across his face. There then gone. His tell: another headache.

"Hey babe, how was work?" he asked.

"Shitty, thanks for asking," I replied, heaving myself on the couch next to him. "But enough about me," I said, giving him a light tap on his shoulder. "How was your appointment? I've been thinking about it all day. Tell me everything!"

He gave me an appraising look, lingering on my boobs. "Well, hello there."

I waved my hand in front of his face and snapped my fingers. "Focus. The appointment; how was it?"

Shawn stood and kissed my forehead, then retreated to the kitchen. Thanks to our open concept layout, living room opened into the kitchen, and we could still chat. He grabbed something from the oven and stood up, proudly presenting me with a burger and fries. My mouth watered.

"Here's your food, babe. I asked for extra sauce on both, so you'll be extra stinky tonight." He gave me an endearing smile; brown eyes crinkling and made his way back to me. "Eat. You're probably starving."

Gratefully, I tore into the burger. Heaven exploded over my tastebuds, and I fought the urge to make a noise more suited for the bedroom. "Thanks, babe," I mumbled through a mouthful.

Shawn folded his long legs underneath him and sat back down. Cracked his knuckles. "The appointment went well," he said, grabbing a can of beer off the coffee table. He took a swig and his Adam's apple bobbed. "Dr. Absinthe was cool and... well... she thinks she can help me."

"That's amazing!" I exclaimed.

"It'll be a big commitment. She wants me to move there."

"Wait, what? Move there? To Denver?" I wasn't expecting that. "Why?"

He rubbed the back of his neck. "The chip isn't FDA-approved—not yet anyway. Dr. Absinthe said the risks were minimal..." Shawn pulled something from his pocket and handed it to me. A brochure. On the front was a chip radiating soothing blue waves. "But since it's still experimental, she wants me to relocate for six months for monitoring. She doesn't expect any problems but said that she'd rather have me close so she can manage any issues if they pop up."

I thumbed through the brochure. On the first page was a list of complications: pain at the insertion site, infection, disability, death—standard stuff for any medical procedure. The next page showed a cartoonish head and a scalpel with the same chip floating just above it. Pointing to the back of my head, I asked, "The chip goes where exactly?"

Shawn pointed to his occiput. "Back here, she said. She doesn't even have to put me out for it but said she'd give me some medicine for my 'nerves.'" He made quotation marks with his fingers.

"That's it?" I was kind of surprised. I figured they'd have to implant it in the skull or something. Being an ER nurse, I'd seen some crazy shit; almost saw it with Shawn as the patient but he'd made it to the OR in time. I'd seen neurosurgeons drilling holes in skulls at the bedside to relieve skyrocketing intracranial pressure, shunts inserted directly into squishy pink brain. Blood. So much of blood. I'd seen it all.

"Yep. Right in her office," he answered.

I considered. Shawn suffered each day since we'd met. First, it was the aftermath of surgery and post-op recovery. Then daily headaches. He couldn't do most of the things he loved. Playing basketball was out of the question; the noise of the ball slapping the floor made the roots of his teeth ache. Plus, he avoided any activities that could result in another head injury. He didn't want to end up like one of those football players with chronic traumatic encephalopathy that lost their minds. How many cancelled dates while Shawn laid in bed, retching into an emesis basin? Too many to count. If Dr. Absinthe could help Shawn... what was six months? If she could fix the love of my life...

Giving him a smile, I said, "If this is what you want to do, I'll follow you to the ends of the Earth. You know that. I can find a job anywhere. Travel nursing is paying good money these days too you know."

Shawn's face brightened, completely transforming. "Oh! And Dr. Absinthe said she knows some folks who might be able to help you out with a job at her hospital system." He looked bashful. "I told her you were an ER nurse."

"That's great!" I exclaimed, although for whatever reason, a kernel of anxiety bloomed in my gut. I pushed it aside; no use in worrying. Setting my food on the table, I walked over to Shawn and wrapped my arms around him.

He rested his head on mine and kissed my hair, murmuring, "Everything is going to change now, babe."

"Yes, it is," I replied.

9

Shawn

THE NEXT WEEK PASSED in a whirlwind. Rachel let her manager know we were relocating for the next six months. They were sad to see her go—she was a kick ass nurse—but understood. *You'll always have a position here,* they said. With Dr. Absinthe's help, we found a nice apartment in Denver that overlooked the bustling downtown. If we desired, we could walk to Coors Field for a Rockies game then pop over to Elitch Gardens—not that I would ever get on a roller-coaster; my brain might explode—ending the day at a trendy restaurant. And after the six months were up, we planned to return to Austin. Thankfully, I wasn't like most athletes. Rather than blowing money on fast cars and women—other than the one time—I invested and accumulated a nice nest egg. We outright owned our house and six months' rent on an apartment was a drop in the bucket. Truthfully, Rachel didn't have to work at all, she wanted to—even if her job drove her crazy sometimes.

Depositing the last box in our crammed trunk, I closed it—barely—and got in the car. We only needed clothes and other odds-and-ends. The apartment came fully furnished.

Rachel climbed into the driver's seat and adjusted the rearview mirror. "You ready for an adventure?" she asked.

I put sunglasses on, hoping to stave off a wicked headache brought on by bright sunlight reflecting off passing windshields. "I was born ready, babe," I replied.

Rachel pointed. "You're seriously bringing *that*?"

"What?"

She gestured with her chin. "That. Your ring. Kind of... ostentatious, isn't it?"

"Ostentatious, huh? That's a big word." I glanced down at my finger, at my NBA Championship ring. She had a point: it was rather big and gaudy; ringed with diamonds. Hefty too. "I dunno. I saw it sitting on the dresser and it felt... right. Taking a little bit of the Old Me to meet the New Me or something."

Rachel leaned over and patted my hand. "As long as it makes you happy, my love. You ready?"

I nodded and we were off; a fifteen-hour drive, excluding stops. I dozed on and off while Rachel drove, waking only when she stopped for a pee break halfway through the journey. She gently shook my shoulder, pulling me out of a half dream: an old standard where I forgot my uniform before an important game—a close cousin to the ol' forgetting your pants for a class presentation. Nothing quite as fun as anxiety dreams.

She asked, "Hey, you want anything to eat or drink?"

Groaning, I opened my eyes and blinked owlishly, adjusting to the light. Green fluorescent lightning from the sign splashed my forearms; she'd parked in front of the gas station. People milled around inside. Most were lined up at the counter while one pimply-faced teenager studied hot dogs rolling in a machine with avid interest. I stretched my legs out. Stiff and achy.

"I'll come in with you. Walking would do me some good. Might as well take a leak too."

"Walking prevents blood clots," she remarked, ever the nurse.

I replied, "So you say."

We got out and held hands walking in. The automatic doors whooshed open, and a blast of cool air washed over us, providing some respite from the scorching heat.

Rachel squeezed my hand. "I'm gonna go pee. My back teeth are floating."

"Okay, hon," I replied. "I'm gonna grab us some snacks. You want anything in particular?"

"Surprise me," she said, scurrying off to the bathroom.

Eyes on the candy selection, I replied, "Roger that." I had an awful sweet tooth. During high school, coach expressly forbid pop and candy, saying it would slow us down on the court. My parents echoed that sentiment, and I was force-fed leafy greens and healthy grains during adolescence. Funnily enough in the NBA, no one gave a shit about our diet as long as we weren't indulging in coke—the drug, not the drink. And if we indulged, it better be out of our system when drug testing came around. I never popped positive so I must have been done something right. I studied the shelves: Skittles, Snickers, Airheads... the possibilities were endless. I grabbed a bag of Tropical Skittles; invariably Rachel ate the ones I didn't like which made our union a match made in heaven.

"Hey mister!"

I turned my head and saw the pimply teen I'd spied studying the ancient hotdogs. A sheen of grease decorated his forehead, and he smelled like stale cabbage farts. Typical.

"Yeah?" The Skittles bag crinkled in my hand.

"Are you Shawn Gilbert?" he asked, exposing teeth gleaming with hardware and rubber bands. He wore a hopeful expression that was easy enough to read; he hoped he'd return to school with a story about meeting someone famous, maybe avoiding another swirly thanks to his brief touch with fame.

"Yeah, I'm Shawn Gilbert," I replied.

His eyes brightened and a grin stretched chapped lips. "Holy shit, no way! I thought it might be you... I saw your ring and thought: *no way, that can't be him!* But it is you! I used to watch your games when I was little." He paused and added, "I loved your movie." Ugh. That fucking movie. About a year after the accident, my agent came to me with the opportunity of a lifetime or so he said.

Despite the headaches and continued physical therapy, I was doing as well as someone with a life-threatening brain bleed post craniotomy could—physically anyway. But mentally? I was deep in the throes of depression. I'd lost my career and a major part of my identity. There's a saying, *basketball is life* and it had been the only life I'd ever known. Gone, just like that. So, I'd agreed to the opportunity of a lifetime. Big mistake. The movie sucked. Imagine *Space Jam* except shitty and filled with rip-off Looney Tunes characters suffering from nuclear radiation. It won a Razzie if that tells you anything.

"Uh, thanks," I said. "It's always nice to meet fans."

"Listen... can I get an autograph?" the kid asked eagerly.

"Of course," I replied. "Uh... you got a pen?" I'd long stopped carrying one with me, especially after leaving enough of them in pockets and running 'em through the wash, much to Rachel's chagrin. With the dexterity of a magician pulling a rabbit from a hat, the kid produced a pen from his shirt pocket and snatched a napkin off the counter.

"Thank you so much!" he gushed.

Scrawling my signature, I handed the pen and napkin back, cringing when his sweaty palm brushed against mine. "Here you go. Thanks for being a fan," I said: my standard line.

"You're the man, Shawn Gilbert!" he exclaimed. "I don't care what my dad says, you're not a pussy."

"What?" I asked. My heart sank and a nugget of irritation bloomed.

He shook his head. "My dad said you faked your injury. Said you were washed up and it was the easy way out to retirement." My blood started to boil. Seeing the expression on my face, the kid quickly added, "My dad's an asshole though. Fuck him."

Ready to unleash a scathing retort, I opened my mouth. "Well—"

"Babe I'm back! What'd you get me?" Rachel said, hooking her arm through mine. Seeing I had company, she gave the kid a polite wave.

My anger deflated at her touch. "Skittles," I replied, handing her the bag.

"Yum! My favorite. I'm gonna grab a Coke, you want anything?"

My jaw clenched. "Yeah, lemme come with you." Rachel pulled me towards the massive fridges lining the back of the gas station.

"Nice to meet you!" the kid called out to my retreating back. I offered a limp wave without looking back.

Rachel inclined her head. "Looks like you met a friend."

"Something like that," I muttered, trying to put the kid's words out of my mind. We purchased our snacks and piled back in the car. We drove in silence for a few miles before Rachel broke the quiet:

"Are you okay?" She shot me a concerned glance. An 18-wheeler roared by, sending up a cloud of exhaust.

"I'm fine," I replied, taking a bite of my Twinkie, chasing it with a swig of Pepsi. While it wasn't exactly the truth, I knew that things were going to get better.

Dr. Absinthe's chip was going to change my life.

I couldn't wait.

10

Shawn

W E STOPPED IN AMARILLO for the night. Rachel couldn't resist singing that terrible country song with the same name as we passed the billboard welcoming visitors to town.

"Who even sings that?" I asked. "Besides my little songbird, I mean." I was more into rap and hip-hop, favoring beats by Jay-Z and Lil Wayne.

Rachel batted her eyes. "You're the worst Texan I've ever met, babe. That's George Strait."

I shook my head and shrugged.

"Seriously, you don't know George Strait?" she asked incredulously.

"Sorry, hon. We didn't play country music when I was growing up." And thank God. I hated whiny country shit.

"Not that you remember, but this song was playing at the nurses' station when I came to visit you that first time," Rachel replied, giving me a coy look.

Rolling my eyes, I replied, "Lucky for me I was mostly unconscious then."

She playfully punched my shoulder.

"Ow! That hurt!" I said, rubbing my arm.

Taking the first exit that boasted hotels—not motels—she replied, "Oh please, like I could hurt a big strong man like you." Pulling up to a stop sign, she glanced over at me. "Do you remember me stopping by to visit you that first time?"

I sighed. "Do we gotta do this every time?"

"Come on, indulge me. It makes me happy," she said, putting on her best pout. I hated when she did that. Mostly because it always worked on me.

"*Fine*, we'll take a little journey down memory lane. *Again*." I didn't remember much from the first days of my hospital stay having been sedated to within an inch of my life, but I remembered her. How could I not? "I remember coming to and seeing you sitting by my bedside." She'd dozed off, head bobbing, an open paperback in her lap. "At first, I thought I'd died or that I was hallucinating but then the pain roared through my head, and I realized that I—unfortunately—was still alive."

Her lips pressed into a thin line, and she replied, "That's what woke me up: your bellyaching."

"Bellyaching? I just had brain surgery!" I protested.

"Teasing babe, teasing." Pulling into the Holiday Inn parking lot, she shifted into park.

"I just figured you visited all your patients when they got admitted," I said.

She laughed. "Not even close. You were the exception." She killed the engine and opened the car door, flooding the interior with light. "I hate to say it Mr. Gilbert, but there was something about you."

I grinned. "That's what my Ma says too."

I grabbed our overnight bag while Rachel checked us in. After a steamy shower, we collapsed into bed. No funny business, we were both too tired. Almost instantly, Rachel's soft snores filled the room. I don't know if it was her nursing career or what, but the woman could fall asleep at the drop of a hat. Not me. Not since the injury.

Back in the day, I passed out immediately, exhausted by all the training and traveling but post-brain injury, I had difficulty calming my mind and spent hours staring up at the ceiling, thinking about life. Sighing, I turned over and stared at the air conditioning unit. Its rattling reminded me of that awful hospital stay, all the myriad of machines whirring. Rachel had been the only bright spot.

Turning up on her days off, she read aloud to me, usually from her chosen smut of the week, grinning wickedly when she got to the naughty bits. *Check out that heart rate*, she'd crow when my monitor alarmed. Eventually she helped with my meals because my hands shook, barely able to navigate a spoon without ending up wearing the food.

She stopped just short of bed baths and dressing me but probably would have if given the chance, but I had to draw the line somewhere. I didn't want her first time seeing me naked be in the hospital, potentially the most unsexy place alive unlike what *Grey's Anatomy* would lead one to think. When they discharged me, I stopped by the hospital gift shop and bought a dozen roses. I thought of the tears in her eyes, the smile on her face when I handed her the flowers. Love filled me.

"Will you go out with me? Since you saved my life and all?" I asked her at the nurses' station while everyone looked on.

"Of course," she replied, her cheeks pinking up. Like a total cliché, everyone clapped, as if we were starring in a romantic comedy. Then, she stood up on her tiptoes, and wrapped her arms around me.

I remembered thinking *this is it*.

Still felt that way.

Turning away from the air conditioner, I sought her out, wrapping my arms around her. She burrowed her face into my chest and sighed in her sleep. A warm drowsiness overcame me and within seconds, I'd followed her to the land of dreams.

11

Dr. Absinthe

I DRIFTED INTO THE breakroom—a hot vanilla latte with oat milk on my mind. A far cry from the beverages of my medical school days—black coffee swigged from Styrofoam cups, sweetened with one sugar and no creamer, the grounds getting caught in my teeth as I went over my SOAP notes with a fine-toothed comb. Not a problem with the new gadget in the breakroom—handier than a Starbucks barista, it brewed a mean cup of coffee, steamed cappuccinos, and dispensed high-octane espressos. The steady influx of money and word-of-mouth had served me well and it was one of my first splurges. I pushed a sequence of buttons and stood back as the machine whirred to life.

"Hey, Aldea," Claire said as she walked in. "You got a sec?"

I turned from the overpriced but fantastic coffee maker. "Yeah, what's up?"

"I just got a phone call from Mrs. Combs' PCP," she said quietly. "Not good news."

Taking in her pinched expression, my heart fluttered. "Okay... you're freaking me out; how about you just tell me what's going on?"

She exhaled loudly. "Mrs. Combs got into a car accident—well... a bus accident..."

"Holy shit!"

Ignoring my outburst, she continued, "That's not the worst of it, Aldea. She was driving a school bus. A *full* school bus."

"That's not good," I said lamely, my heart sinking.

"Don't worry, it gets worse. She drove the bus off a bridge into the Colorado River."

I hissed through my teeth. "Shit..." I imagined the frothy white currents and my stomach turned. Perfect conditions for white water rafting, not so much for a runaway bus. Those relentless currents pulling tiny bodies to frozen depths, submerging them while lungs filled insidiously with fluid.

"Yeah, shit is a proper response," Claire replied.

"Are—are the kids—?" I started, afraid of the answer.

Claire slowly shook her head. "Deader than shit. If they didn't die of trauma secondary to the crash, they drowned. Can you imagine? Dying in a bright ass yellow tomb like that? Fucking awful."

I placed my hand over my mouth. "I can't believe it, that's unreal." Unprovoked, I thought of Mrs. Combs' smiling face transforming into a silent scream as her waterlogged body bloated; white pruned fingers giving way to rot.

"Yeah, well. Her doc also sent over an autopsy report over for her. I put it on your desk for you to look at later." Claire gave me a meaningful look and squeezed my shoulder. "I just wanted you to know. Sorry to put a damper on your day."

What would they find—if anything? The woman was middle aged; healthy enough but a career in medicine taught me we all had a ticking time bomb inside of us waiting to go off. But because she was my patient, with one of my not FDA-approved chips in her—I worried.

"It's okay, I get it. Shit happens, right?" I said, trying to convince myself more than anything. Even though being a doctor meant you had to develop a certain familiarity with death, it didn't make it any easier when confronted with it.

Claire gave me a curt nod. "Right. Now get your caffeine in. We've got a big day ahead."

"Yeah, we do. No rest for the wicked," I said to her retreating back. Nothing like hearing about a patient death to start the day out. "Dammit," I whispered. Steam burst from the machine and I jumped, my heart rate skyrocketing. "Jesus!"

"Dr. Absinthe, how's that kitty of yours?" Billie asked, peeking her head through the breakroom door, further scaring the shit out of me. Pink highlights streaked through her black mane, a change from the white ones she sported last month. The pink contrasted well with her dark skin. Billie flirted with a goth aesthetic that worked for her.

"Oh, he's better. The cast came off last week," I replied, trying to play it cool like a machine and my receptionist hadn't scared the living daylights out of me in rapid succession. "Thanks for asking."

The cast coming off was a huge relief. The vet—Dr. Adams—assured me Spooky wouldn't mess with his casted leg which was covered in neon green material purported to deter pets from chewing, thoughtfully named: No Chew. Even though it was—allegedly—bitter, Spooky acquired a taste for the stuff and tore through four casts in rapid succession. Not that it was all terrible—his vet was pretty darn cute.

On our fifth visit I joked, "Are you rubbing rotisserie chicken on it back there? So you can see me again?"

Dr. Adams' dimples appeared. "You've caught on to my dastardly master plan." She put her hands on her hips. "Maybe I need to pay for my boat, did you ever think of that? A girl's gotta make money somehow."

"Do you have a boat?" I asked.

"Nope," Dr. Adams replied, shaking her head, a playful glint in her eyes. Her black curls caught the light.

I shrugged. "Well... we're practically dating at this point, so..." I trailed off and smiled. She'd laughed at my dumb jokes before and displayed what I considered *potential lesbian eye-contact—gaze* lingering a second too long, then dropping to my lips. Women that liked women were *notorious* for that move.

"If we're practically dating... then why haven't you asked me out yet?" she asked.

I couldn't help my involuntary goofy grin but held it together long enough to ask her just that. And as it turned out, my gaydar—for once—was spot on. After work today we were meeting at a local brewery and my mind cycled through my wardrobe. Jeans? What did one wear on their first date with their cat's veterinarian? A cat shirt?

"Saw the schedule for this afternoon," Billie said conspiratorially, pulling me out of my thoughts. She leaned her thin frame against the door and her eyes gleamed. "I hear he's famous," she said in a singsong voice.

I grabbed my latte and took a sip. Perfect. Heat rolled down my throat. "I assume you're talking about Shawn Gilbert?" I asked. It certainly wasn't Jeffrey Hausen—my two o'clock, an elderly creep who used his Parkinson's tremor as an excuse to brush against women's bodies. *So terribly sorry about that*, he'd say, a lecherous smile accompanying his words.

Billie playfully rolled her eyes. "Duh, Shawn Gilbert! Claire told me he was some big shot, so I stalked him online. Very cute."

I narrowed my eyes. "What do you know about Shawn Gilbert, Billie? Are you going to go all *Swimfan* on me right now?" Remembering movies from the 2000s was much better than thinking of Mrs. Combs' fate.

"What's that?" she asked.

"You don't know about *Swimfan*?"

Billie's eyes were blank, and she gave a slight shake of her head.

"It's a movie about a woman who becomes obsessed with this high school swimmer. Stalking and all that. She goes a bit... fucking nuts." I'd only watched it a billion times, mostly due to Erika Christensen's portrayal of a hot psychopath—in my youth, I'd gravitated towards the unhinged ones for whatever reason. I loved a walking red flag. Emphasis on the past tense.

Billie shrugged. "I saw all the pics of him, Shawn Gilbert's a fox. Look at him! Those brown eyes, that tan?" Billie put the back of her hand to her forehead and pretended to swoon. "A bonafide fox," she added, waving herself with an imaginary fan with the other hand.

She wasn't wrong... Shawn Gilbert was easy on the eyes, if you were into that tall handsome basketball player sort of thing.

"Yes... but that's not all he is," I said, tightly gripping my cup. Heat seeped into my palm. "He's my generation's Michael Jordan."

"Who?"

I snapped my head around. "You *seriously* don't know who Michael Jordan is?"

"I've heard his name," she replied defensively.

Sipping my coffee, I reconsidered. How old was Billie? 22? Maybe. A fetus practically compared to my old ass. "He was like... LeBron James," I said.

"Oh." Understanding bled into her expression. "So, Shawn Gilbert was a big deal?"

I nodded. "Definitely. Unstoppable on the court. Destined to break records but..." I trailed off.

"The accident," Billie said, adding, "I read his *Wikipedia* page and watched the video on *YouTube*. Ouch."

I'd seen it happen in real time; my eyes glued to the screen as it unfolded. How he fell woodenly to the polished floor, knocked out cold. The camera zoomed in on worried teammates hovering over his stiff form, referees calling for a medic with increasingly alarmed tones. Then, Shawn's limbs violently clenched and his head whipped back. The movement became rhythmic: a seizure.

I'd only been in my teens—lightyears away from medical school and my neurology residency—but instinctively I recognized: *This was not gonna be good.* And I was right. A near life-ending injury which claimed his career and eventually, his sanity. *Devastating brain injury*, the internet proclaimed. Having reviewed his medical chart, I saw he'd suffered from an intracranial hemorrhage due to a splintered temporal bone and his brain swelled from the trauma. He bought himself a ventilator and a series of surgeries. Surprisingly, he emerged still able to walk and talk, with lots of physical therapy of course.

A miracle, truth be told.

"Yeah, the accident. We're going to insert his chip today," I added, tipping my coffee towards her. "Needed an extra hit of caffeine before I cut into a world-famous athlete."

Billie twirled her rose gold nose ring and asked, "How much coffee did you drink before you did mine?"

"Like three shots of espresso. I stayed up late watching scary movies and needed the extra focus."

"Comforting," Billie said. "But like Dr. Water's wife says after sex: wow, I didn't feel a thing!"

I groaned.

"Get it? Because Dr. Waters is an anesthesiologist?" Billie asked.

"I get it, Billie. Probably not inaccurate either."

Are you nervous?" Billie asked.

I kept my face neutral. "Eh, not really," I lied.

12

Shawn

I SAT ON A chair just inside the door and gazed around the procedure room. Gowned up and freezing. Again. Gleaming instruments rested on blue towels, winking under the fluorescents. Some familiar—scalpels and forceps—while others appeared vaguely sinister; they'd be right at home in a deranged dentist's office. One tool had razor sharp teeth that looked as if they'd been extracted from the mouth of a dinosaur from *Jurassic Park*. An image flitted through my head: Dr. Absinthe sawing into my skull, liberating a square piece of bone, her white-gloved finger poking my brain. I shivered and pushed the weird daydream away. *C'mon... she's not a psychopath in a horror movie*, I admonished myself. In the middle of the room, was a table; like the ones I'd seen in massage therapists' offices. Far more expensive and sophisticated though, evidenced by the countless peddles and buttons adorning its sides.

Knock, knock, knock.

The wooden door shook in its frame at the three quick raps administered to it. A brief second passed and then—without waiting for an invitation—a slender, weasel-faced man dressed in blue scrubs burst in. His shoes squeaked as he abruptly halted.

Gazing through thick-framed glasses, he studied me—like a kid might examining a marginally interesting insect.

"Hello, Mr. Gilbert? I'm Dr. Waters, your anesthesiologist," he said, giving an awkward limp-wristed wave in the way of greeting. I knew better than to offer my hand. He was either too germophobic or on the spectrum to handle such things, that much was obvious.

"Uh... hi. I'm Shawn... Gilbert. But you already knew that." I said lamely. My cheeks burned.

Dr. Waters nodded and slapped the table. "Hop on." Once on the table, Dr. Waters bombarded me with questions I'd answered at least eighty times on varying pieces of paperwork. Seemingly satisfied, he grasped my hand and started an IV. He slapped stickers on my chest, clipping multicolored leads to the metal button in the middle of each, plugging the whole mess into a monitor just above my head. The anesthesiologist's rheumy eyes watered and after his pen finishing skittering, he wiped them impatiently. Then, without another word, Dr. Waters whirled and left the room.

"Okaayyyyy. What the fuck?" I mumbled. Dr. Waters' bedside manner, while not completely appalling—he hadn't stuck his finger up my ass without consent or anything—was severely lacking. Probably why he'd picked anesthesia: the unconscious possessed minimal social skills.

I intertwined my fingers and cracked my knuckles, wishing Rachel were here. Dr. Absinthe offered to let Rachel sit in on the procedure and she'd declined. "Oh no," Rachel said. "Respectfully, I know that the last thing you want is a nurse watching your every movement like a hawk. I'd rather you be nice and relaxed the whole time." Not that I could blame her; she wanted everything to go perfectly. But... it would have been nice to feel her hand within mine—a warm, comforting presence telling me, *everything will be okay.*

Knock, knock.

A polite pause, unlike Dr. Waters earlier.

"Come in!" I called.

The door opened and Dr. Absinthe strolled in. A regal air followed her; instead of a doctor, she was a famous supermodel strutting her stuff on the catwalk. Flattering blue scrubs—likely custom fitted and tailored if I had to guess—hugged her curves. She looked like one of the sexy residents Rachel watched on *Grey's Anatomy*. She'd pulled her hair into a tight bun and wore a scrub cap patterned with smiling black cats. A hint of her brunette hair peeked out.

She offered her hand to me, warmly shaking with a much better handshake than her cohort. "Hi, Shawn. Are you ready for the procedure that will change your life?" She smiled. A faint hint of perfume washed over me—not floral or overpowering. Just right.

"As ready as I'll ever be," I replied through a bad case of cotton mouth. Partly from nerves, but mostly because I hadn't had a sip of water since washing down the Valium Rachel handed me before we left... not strictly on Dr. Absinthe's orders. *You need to chill out babe*, she said. She wasn't wrong.

Dr. Absinthe replied, "Excellent." Winking at me, she said, "Don't worry, it'll be a *slam dunk*."

I groaned, not that it wiped the smirk from her face.

"Sorry. I couldn't help myself. I gotta take the jokes when they present themselves," she said.

Dr. Waters reentered the room, clutching a vial of milky white medicine. He offered a caveman grunt to Dr. Absinthe and disappeared behind my head. Plastic crinkled and something clinked against glass.

"Listen, Shawn—" Dr. Absinthe started. I turned my attention to her. She'd put on a facemask and kind brown eyes gazed at me. "Dr. Waters is going to inject some medication into your IV. You'll start feeling sleepy and I promise: you won't remember a *thing*. The medicine burns a little, but you should feel *great* in a few seconds. I tell people to picture their happy place. Maybe a beach with a frosty beer in your hand?" She paused, adding, "Of course... that might be *my* happy place!"

I replied, "No, the beach is good."

I leaned back and closed my eyes. White sands beckoned. Birds called out in exotic tongues. Waves broke against the beach, flavoring the warm air with salt. Sun beat down, sending an electric tingle through my exposed skin. Nope—nothing wrong with a beach. Burning bloomed in my IV, roaring into my veins. The sensation crawled up my arm, like a match setting fire to skin. Around me, the room wavered and swam. My vision shrunk to a pinhole and went black. I had enough time to think, *it's time.*

And it was.

13

Dr. Absinthe

THE PROCEDURE WENT WONDERFULLY. Textbook even. Not that I'd written about my chips in any such tomes or medical journals. Not yet. Once Dr. Waters gave Shawn the juice and he drifted off, I started my work. Shawn didn't necessarily need procedural sedation but after having patients move around on me, I always offered it. Billie went for it when I did her chip and after coming out of it told me, "That wasn't as fun as the Ketamine drip a doc tried for my migraines a few times but still cool."

I performed a quick nerve block—occipital—that I'd practiced many times; injected the anesthetic and waited for it to take effect. Another reason I'm an anomaly for a neurologist. My specialty wasn't really known for procedural prowess. Gone were the days where we performed lumbar punctures—they were now outsourced to interventional radiology. But I performed nerve blocks all the time—they helped with certain neuralgias, sometimes with headaches, but even more so? I got to bill for it. Procedures meant more money.

Setting my needle and syringe down, I clutched an 11-blade scalpel and created a small nick at the base of Shawn's skull. I wiped the dark blood welling up from the wound with a 4x4 gauze. Bluntly dissecting through tissue using my gloved finger,

I pinpointed the spot, feeling the curve of his skull. "Bingo," I said aloud to myself. Dr. Waters didn't even peer over the drape; he'd gotten used to me talking to myself.

With thin-needled tweezers, I grabbed the chip and relocated it to its new home: Shawn Gilbert's head. Tweezers were exchanged for hemostats, and I sutured the incision closed.

"Waters, I can handle the rest of this if you want to split," I offered, hoping he took me up on the offer. At baseline, he drove me fucking crazy. I suspected he had undiagnosed ADHD or a mild form of autism. Or he was just annoying. When charting, he drummed his fingers on the Mayo stand—rattling medication vials until I wanted to scream—and I often dreamed of plunging a needle loaded with potent poison into his carotid or strangling him to death.

Already to his feet, Dr. Waters said, "You got it, boss. Thanks a lot!" and was out the door in a flash. The only time he moved with any sort of urgency was after clocking out or when going on break. Otherwise, his standard speed was a slow amble. I half expected to see a cloud of dust in his wake. I watched the door settle and drew up an additional dose of Propofol... just in case. This wasn't my first rodeo and while most people did fine with the sedation, some were absolute bears. I'd had two patients emerge from the procedure full on psychotic and Shawn Gilbert was a big boy. Even retired, he could tear me limb from limb if he so pleased. That's why I liked a little extra insurance and the loaded syringe felt comforting in my hand.

I glanced up. His vitals were great. The monitor cheerfully beeped with each heartbeat, slow and steady. Shawn's chest rose and fell—breathing on his own. Always a plus. Sometimes Propofol rendered people apneic, requiring prompt intervention—look at Michael Jackson's whole debacle—and sometimes even intubation. I wasn't planning on that today. Peeling my sterile gloves off and depositing them in the trash, I walked to my laptop propped open on the counter. Quickly, I skimmed the screen and peered at Shawn once more.

Still out.

I picked out a succession of letters, coaxing the chip to life. Shortly thereafter, it would start inhibiting the neurons responsible for the debilitating pain response that blossomed into monster migraines. The layer of skull didn't damper its effect at all, a blessing. If it had, this procedure would be a lot more invasive, maybe even requiring a piece of skull to be cut away. And that certainly wouldn't be happening in an office, more like an operating room with a neurosurgeon.

My pinky tapped the ENTER button.

Shawn's eyes shot open, but face and body remained slack.

Good.

No sudden movements or outbursts.

His wooden gaze found me, and I marveled at how dilated his pupils were—completely incongruent with the brightly lit procedure room. I hit another key—the last in the sequence—and shut the laptop with a snap. I stood in front of Shawn, waiting for the light in his eyes to return. Seconds passed. His stare softened and facial muscles relaxed. Lines ironed themselves out. He blinked slowly and a look of confusion twisted his features.

Groggily he asked, "Ugh—is—did—you give me... medicine yet?"

I chuckled and said, "Shawn, we're all done! You did great, no issues. How do you feel? How's the headache?" Without moving, I observed him, fully prepared to bolt at any sudden movements.

Shawn reached up and gently probed his scalp with his fingers. "I... my headache." His eyebrows shot up. "It's gone! Gone!" Excitement made his voice's pitch high, like a teenager in the throes of puberty. "It's gone! Can you believe it?" Tears gathered and threatened to spill over his long eyelashes.

Watching patients realize that their life had changed, that I'd healed them—

It was the reason I became a doctor; healing someone almost functioned as an addiction for me. You made a person feel better, enriching their lives, and they repaid you with genuine gratitude.

It felt good knowing all the years of hard work and sacrifice were worth it. And not that I would admit this to anyone; especially not someone involved with medicine but while practicing, helping, sometimes even curing people—I've never felt such a feeling of power. I imagined it was what surgical specialties felt; why they so often had the so-called God Complex. I understood it. I'd intervened on a debilitating condition, using my talents and intelligence, with a dash of daring. My inhibiting chip was something new, something novel. The first of its kind. My job satisfaction had never been higher.

Nor had the stakes.

"You're very welcome. Didn't I tell you? Slam dunk, am I right?" I said.

Shawn gushed, "I just can't believe it! Wow." He stood and extended his arms. "Not to be awkward but—can I give you a hug?"

"Of course! I love a good hug," I replied, holding my arms out. A sprig of fire leaped into my chest; *Shawn Gilbert*—my childhood idol—was going to hug *me*. Middle school me would have hyperventilated herself into syncope while wearing her Adidas tracksuit.

He pulled me into a tight embrace hug and as short as I was, my ear rested against his chest, and I heard his heart thudding away. Fast. Excited. "Thank you," he murmured softly.

"You ready to get out of here?" I asked, pulling away from him. "I bet your wife is dying to see you."

With a wide grin, he responded, "Absolutely."

Claire poked her head in. "Everything going okay?"

"More than okay," I answered, gesturing at a visibly elated Shawn, nearly shaking with happiness. "I think he's ready for you."

"Perfect!" Claire said. She gently grasped Shawn's forearm. "Follow me and we'll get you squared away. Let me know if you feel nauseated or anything." Shawn nodded his assent and allowed her to guide him from the room.

Watching them exit, my smile ebbed. With Shawn's procedure out of the way... I had no excuse to not look at Mrs. Combs' autopsy report.

I worried what I might find.

14

Rachel

T HE NURSE—CLAIRE—HANDED SHAWN A cup of water and watched as he slowly drank. "Crackers next," she said, handing him three packages of saltines. No matter where I'd worked, the drawers were stocked with saltines or graham crackers. I sometimes wondered if Big Cracker had an agreement with all healthcare institutions or if the whole medical establishment somehow agreed that saltines and graham crackers were the way to go.

Shawn ripped the crackers open. Claire was putting Shawn through his paces after his procedural sedation. You had to make sure your patient could walk of their own volition, could drink and eat without barfing, and had a sober ride. We also told them not to elope in Vegas or buy a car. People liked to blame poor decisions on anything other than their own stupidity... so we had to administer such warnings and document them—or risk a massive lawsuit later.

Shawn made short work of the crackers. "Easy peasy," he said, giving Claire a grin as if to say, *look how well I'm doing!*

"Alright then, how about you get up and walk for me?" Claire said.

Shawn shot up out of the chair and strode across the room. He reached the wall and turned, clicking his sock-covered heels together in a passable Dorothy impression—the only things missing were the ruby red heels and adorable dog. "See that? I'm perfectly recovered!" he crowed. I believed it. In the span of an hour, years had dropped from his face. The fine lines around his mouth and brow receded, leaving smooth skin behind.

"Yes, you are. Cute little dance move or whatever that was too," Claire replied and scribbled something in his chart. "Maybe you'll have a career on *Dancing with the Stars* soon. We'll see you back here tomorrow for your post-op check, okay?"

"Sounds good to me," Shawn replied. We didn't speak until getting into the car. I slipped behind the steering wheel and turned the key. The engine roared to life. "Babe—" Shawn said, grabbing my forearm.

"What? Is everything okay?" I asked.

My heart rate spiked. Wife brain roared to the forefront, pushing everything I knew about nursing away. "What's wrong?"

Shawn shook his head. "That's the thing—nothing's wrong. Look." He pointedly looked at me and rotated his neck side-to-side. "I can move my neck without a headache. The tightness in my shoulders—completely gone." Awe filled his voice.

Completely contrary to my bad bitch persona—cultivated after years toiling in the trenches of the hospital—I burst into tears.

15

Shawn

"Back again for more fun?" Billie said.

Week three after the chip insertion and life had never been better.

I leaned against the reception desk. "Yep."

Billie leaned back and typed on her computer. Her black nail polish was chipped, and her eyeliner was smudged.

"Billie?"

"Yeah?" she asked tiredly.

I leaned closer and motioned with my chin. "That guy over there?"

She found him with her eyes. "Yeah?"

"I watched him pick his nose and wipe the boogers in that *Sports Illustrated*."

Billie sighed. Dark circles hung from her eyes—and not from last night's makeup. I knew that look: pure exhaustion. "Thanks for letting me know. People are animals, I swear." Her eyes darted to her computer. "Can't wait for 5 o'clock, I'll tell you that."

I hesitated—*thinking is this my business?*—but asked anyway: "Is everything okay?"

Her gaze darted up and her eyes widened. I noticed the red vessels threading through them. "Yes. I mean, well—I don't know. I guess." I didn't say anything, not wanting to pry. She cracked her knuckles then looked down at her shredded cuticles. "It's just... things aren't going well with Jerry." She quickly added, "My boyfriend. Ex-boyfriend. Whatever."

"I'm sorry."

Billie's shoulders sagged. "He said I'd changed. That I wasn't the same girl he fell in love with. I'm too *temperamental*." She sniffed. "At one point I believe he said: *psychotic*. Me? Psychotic?" Billie's voice rose and patients craned their necks, the nosepicker included.

"Oh," I said dumbly. "You seem fine to me."

She looked at me glumly. "Well, that's gotta stand for something, huh? Shawn Gilbert thinks I'm in perfect mental health!" She let out a barky laugh. "Whatever. His loss, right? I'll make him see."

"Right. His loss," I agreed, privately thinking maybe the guy dodged a bullet.

Billie pushed a green button. "Dr. Absinthe will see you now."

I thanked her and headed back. Entering the office, I sat down in the comfy leather chair across from Dr. Absinthe. Rubbed my fingertips on the expensive feeling wood grain.

"How are things going?" Dr. Absinthe asked. Her white coat fluttered, revealing a stripe of bright yellow. I thought about asking her what Billie's deal was—if she was okay but mentioning it felt... icky. Wasn't everyone entitled to a shitty day? I knew I'd had my fair of 'em.

I smiled and pointed. "I like the yellow."

"What?" she asked. "Oh! My scrubs?" She pinched the material between her fingers and closely inspected it as if seeing them for the first time. "I've always liked yellow. It's a happy color."

"Me too. It was one of my team colors." Purple and yellow.

"That's right! I didn't even think about it when I was getting dressed today." Dr. Absinthe reconsidered and tapped her head with her index finger. "Maybe subconsciously I knew though."

"Yeah, maybe."

"Doing well, then?" she asked.

"Better than well, I'd think," I replied.

A thin smirk played on her lips. "Oh yeah?"

"Definitely," I replied. "I joined a gym again." Previously, the gym had been no-go zone: the clanking plates, grunts and occasional screams when lifting heavy, all the straining? Headache central. Just begging for an aneurysm rupture. "And I'm running again," I added.

Basketball always came first but come spring—the track was my domain. While I had *nowhere* near my father's prowess, I medaled a few times at State. During basketball's off season, I laced up my Nikes and drove out to Lady Bird Lake Trail with downtown Austin in view. Running functioned almost like meditation for me. Calmed the mind. Nothing quite like blasting your favorite music while autumn shook yellowing leaves free, allowing your mind to disengage. Just be. Plus, it kept weight off. After the accident, running too became a no-go. Way too much pounding. Since the procedure, I rediscovered my love for it and headed out on nearby trails; Colorado boasted a ton. New Balance or Saucony could hit me up if they needed a washed-up athlete to rep their brands.

"Very good, very good." Dr. Absinthe nodded. "Any headaches at all?"

"Not a single one," I replied. "Does that chip loosen up muscles too or what?" I'd become accustomed to my shoulders residing up near my ears—and the accompanying neck spasms, debilitating tightening that brought me to my knees.

Dr. Absinthe nodded. "It can," she replied. "Some headaches are secondary to tight musculature: tension headaches. My chip inhibits—inhibit the trigger points, boom; the entire muscle relaxes."

She wasn't kidding. I felt more relaxed than I ever had in my life. I shook my head and said, "Whatever's happening; I feel like a completely new man. Seriously. You're a lifesaver."

She really was. My marriage had never been better. Our sex life? Going at it like newlyweds. As much I hated being *that guy*—too often I had to give the true, but terrible excuse:

Babe not tonight. I've got a headache. When you're living with what doctors deemed status migrainosus or intractable migraines—hanky panky ain't on the menu, despite my best efforts. Now with a clear, pain-free head, I felt like I was back in college. Just this morning before the appointment, I bent her over the kitchen island, sending her off to work with a smile. Our spark was back.

Dr. Absinthe pursed her lips together. "Happy to hear it! And—uh, on that note—I wanted to chat with you. About something." The words tumbled awkwardly from her mouth, and she tapped her fingers on the desk.

Immediately my defenses went up as if she'd said *we need to talk*, my stomach dropping into my ass. "Okay..." I replied. It didn't matter who wanted to talk—wife, girlfriend, chick-on-the-side, Ma, or a doctor—it always sucked. Experience taught me that much.

Unbidden, a memory unearthed itself. Without the maelstrom clouding my thinking—it was happening more and more often. Constant agony ensured I didn't make many trips down memory lane; I'd concerned myself more with surviving the day without blowing my brains out. I remembered after *that* game, when Brynn grasped my sweat slicked bicep and pulled me into the hallway. Through the locker room door, I heard my teammates whooping it up. Celebrating. I ought to be with them, especially after such a huge win.

"What?" I said flatly, scanning the hallway. A few security guards. Nobody I knew. Couldn't she see it was a bad time?

A pained look flitted across Brynn's face and in a low voice she said, "Shawn—we need to talk." Her ensuing words filled with cold dread, rooting me to the spot. Soul left body. And it had every right to.

While whatever Dr. Absinthe had to say could in no way be like the bombshell dropped on me then—it still made me nervous as hell. I pushed the memory from my brain.

Dr. Absinthe stood and walked to the window. Peering out, she said, "You're feeling a lot better, so you agree: the chip works, right?" She rocked on her heels and clasped her hands behind her back.

"Um... *yeah* it works!" I answered.

"Right, right, right," she agreed. Whirling around, she brought the figurative hammer down—hitting me with it: "What-would-you-think-of-being-a-spokesperson-for-the-chip?" Again, the words spilled from her lips.

Then I realized: she was *nervous*. I burst out laughing. Talk about worrying for nothing! "You mean like Shaq with that athlete's foot medicine?" I asked.

Dr. Absinthe laughed and shrugged her shoulders. "I mean... kind of. But this would be much more glamorous than toe fungus obviously." She gestured broadly. "As you know, the chip isn't FDA-approved yet. Maybe in a few years; we'll see. But people could benefit from the chip *now*."

"That's true," I replied. How much had I already benefitted from it? It gave me my life back.

She waved her hand. "I haven't nailed it all down yet but there would be commercials and ads. Who knows—" She waggled her fingers "—maybe a *Good Morning America* interview? *The Show*? Me having someone with your star power in my corner would be a huge help." Her cheeks reddened. "But like, don't feel obligated or anything, okay?" Alarm widened her eyes. "Oh my god, I'm not being weird right now—am I?" Her nostrils flared at her horror of possibly offending me.

I considered her offer: should I? We weren't exactly hurting for money—thanks to smart financial investments; made after I got my shit together—and I didn't really *need* to work. Technically,

Rachel didn't need to work either but despite all her bitching and moaning—she loved her job. But... how long had it been since I'd done anything truly meaningful with my life? Had a purpose other than taking room up on the living room couch, inhaling precious oxygen? Even Make-A-Wish kids didn't want to meet me anymore. No one cared about a washed-up athlete. My sponsorships dried up years ago.

I pulled my phone from my pocket and waved Dr. Absinthe off. "Don't worry! It's not weird. It's actually—" I paused and gathered my thoughts. "—it's awesome." Heat bloomed in my chest: happiness. "At the risk of sounding like a prick," I started. "You're going to need to call my agent about that." How long had it been since I said *that*? I shook my head. "Wow, Dr. Absinthe, this is amazing."

Dr. Absinthe shot me a grin. "Since we're going to work together and all; call me Aldea."

16

Dr. Absinthe

I PORED OVER A medical journal and munched on a steak and cheese panini from the sandwich vendor in the atrium. Turning past yet another article about anti-NMDA receptor encephalitis—a hot topic ever since that *Brain on Fire: My Month of Madness* memoir came out years ago—I wondered when *my name* would grace the pages. Hopefully soon if things continued their present trajectory.

Claire popped her head into the office. "Hey Aldea—I know you're taking your lunch but—"

I swallowed a glob of cheese and waved her in. "It's fine. What's up?"

"Dr. Chase called. He wanted your input on a patient," Claire said. Dr. Chase? Who the hell was Dr. Chase? Catching the bewildered expression on my face, Claire added, "You know... Dr. Chase. The guy who wears suspenders and a pocket protector? Bit of a lisp?"

I snapped my fingers. "Oh yeah! The headcase guy."

"I think they prefer 'psychiatrists' these days."

Waving my hand, I replied, "I know that, Claire. I meant Dr. Chase himself is a headcase. Didn't you see him at last year's Christmas party?"

"You mean when he got sloshed and started yelling about Peace on Earth?" Her eyebrow quirked up.

"Exactly. Don't forget how he toppled the ice sculpture and started sobbing." I clucked my tongue. "The irony of it: the psychiatrist needing a strong anti-psychotic."

She leaned over and handed me a yellow Post-it with a number scrawled on it. "At any rate, he wants you to call him. Sooner rather than later. He sounded a bit... frantic."

"Ugh, *fine*," I replied, rolling my eyes. Claire left and I eyed my sandwich then sighed and picked up the phone. No rest for the wicked as they say. I dialed the number, puzzling over the last digit before deciding it was a 1, not a 7. And they say doctors have terrible handwriting.

Dr. Chase answered on the first ring. "Yes, hello?"

I plastered a fake smile on my face. "Dr. Chase! It's Dr. Absinthe."

"Who?"

"Aldea Absinthe? Neurology?" Silence. I tapped my fingers on the desk. "My nurse said you wanted to talk to me about a patient?" More dead air. "Um—" I started.

He barked out a course laugh, making me tense up in my chair. "Oh yeah! The brain gal!"

I pinched the skin between my eyebrows. "Right, the brain gal. Listen, what do you need?" I glanced longingly at my half-finished panini and open medical journal. "I'm a busy woman as you can imagine so—"

"Of course!" he said, cutting me off. "It might be better to have you come to the psychiatric unit to explain though."

I checked the clock—thirty minutes left in my lunch break. "Fine," I replied, hanging up. Psych wasn't exactly my least favorite rotation in medical school—it was nowhere near as disgusting and bodily fluid laden as OB was—but I didn't relish being around those people: Psychiatrists. Shudder. No one was droller than a psychiatrist. Plus, I always had the sense they were taking mental notes, fitting me somewhere within the pages of the DSM.

I inhaled the rest of my sandwich as I walked to the psychiatric unit. After navigating a gauntlet of locked doors and showing my badge to no less than three security guards and two nurses who could have pommeled me into paste if they so wished, I found myself in Dr. Chase's office, staring at a large velvet painting of Elvis. Where did someone even get something so tacky?

"Aldea! Nice to see you again!" Dr. Chase said, offering me his hand.

I shook it, marveling at how sweaty yet limp it was. A boneless jellyfish. "Likewise." I wrenched my gaze away from the repugnant artwork.

He sat down in his leather chair with a fart noise. "That was—uh—the chair."

"Sure." I mirrored him, sitting down in my chair without any flatulence—real or simulated.

He peered at me through his glasses, eyes freakishly magnified. "Turns out we share a mutual patient."

"Do we now?"

He nodded, disrupting his comb-over. "Indeed. Landis." Dr. Chase stroked his pocket protector unconsciously as he said her name.

I snapped my fingers. "Oh yeah, Aubrey. I saw her last month. She was doing great." More than great. She looked like a completely new woman. Her migraines rendered her unable to sleep more than an hour or two a night and she doped herself up on enough medication to sedate an elephant without any discernable results. Once I put her chip in—a switch flipped, and she slept eight hours a night since. Not one headache.

Dr. Chase's watery gray eyes widened. "Oh... well. Great is not the adjective I'd use when referring to Aubrey right now, I'm afraid. Far from it. More like bad. Very bad." His nose wrinkled as if he found everything about this conversation distasteful.

"Very bad?" I repeated.

"Extremely."

I waited for him to elaborate. "And?"

He jolted. "Oh right! Well, it seems Aubrey had what I would qualify as a psychotic break. Just this afternoon in fact." He shook his head forlornly. "A shame too. I thought I'd gotten her meds just right."

"What happened?" Impatience crawled its way up my throat, and I grit my teeth. I'd be here all day if I had to pull the story out of him like this.

Dr. Chase leaned back, took his glasses off and started polishing them with a dirty cloth pulled from his white collared shirt pocket—tucked behind the row of pens enclosed in his pocket condom for nerds. "Aubrey went to the grocery store today and seems—seems that she got a bit... upset in the checkout line. An elderly woman in front of her at the checkout was taking too long for Aubrey's liking. You see, she was paying in pennies and—well... the cashier said that—" he peered at a written chart on his desk and made air quotes with his fingers "—that, 'she just lost her shit.'" He sniffed. "She also lost control of her bladder at this point. And that was before the police tazed her."

I took a deep breath in and slowly exhaled. "What is it you're wanting from me then? Sounds like a cut and dry psychosis. And if you want my opinion, sounds like it was justified to an extent." I held my hands out. "Paying with pennies? Who does that?"

He wrinkled his nose again, morphing into a peeved bunny rabbit. "Physical violence is never the answer, no matter how frustrated one might be."

I suppressed an urge to roll my eyes. Mr. Manners over here. "Agree to disagree then. What is it I can do for you? Right now. In this very moment." I tapped the desk to emphasize my point.

He picked a piece of lint from his shirt. "Just crossing my t's, dotting my i's. I was reviewing her chart and saw she'd had a procedure with you recently."

"Yeah, I implanted one of my migraine chips but—"

He cut me off, "Anything else? Any new medications? Did she receive any medications in the office to facilitate chip placement?"

I cast my memory back. "Just Lidocaine with epi. I offer most patients procedural sedation, mostly for anxiolysis but she declined. At our post-op visit, she was doing great. No more migraines."

Dr. Chase leaned back in his chair, creating another faint fart noise which we both ignored. "Hmmm... well... I suppose Aubrey had a setback with her mental health then. It happens. I can't imagine the chip is responsible for her behavior. Well... thanks for stopping by. Just wanted to make sure I wasn't overlooking anything," Dr. Chase said, pointedly staring at the door—my cue to exit.

"Sure... let me know if you need anything else," I said, getting up from the chair, my knees faintly protesting. Dr. Chase offered a grunt in reply, and I left. Walking back to my office, I considered: *could* it be the chip? No, surely not.

But something bothered me about the whole thing.

I took the back entrance into the office, found Claire, and pulled her aside.

"Hey, listen. I'll be a little late to my 1 p.m. appointment. Tell them sorry but an emergency came up," I said.

"Everything okay?" Claire asked. "Anything you need me to do?"

"Nah, I just need to check something out. No big deal."

Once back in my office, I pulled up Aubrey's chart and scanned it for any clues, any outlier.

Nothing.

I rubbed my temples and turned the problem over in my mind. The chip worked to inhibit stimuli responsible for pain impulses, effectively blocking them. In theory, the chip could inhibit other signals as well but causing significant changes in personality or impulse control—it seemed less likely but if it were causing such issues...

I'd be in a world of shit.
Once I got back from my trip; I'd sort it out.

17

Dr. Absinthe

THE STUDIO AUDIENCE STARED expectantly at us. I couldn't quite make out individual faces under the blinding stage lighting but heard them murmuring to each other; their anticipation palpable. Off to the side, a woman—wearing a perpetual frown and headphones—gestured to the hosts and shouted: "One minute!" My throat tightened and I tried to slow my breathing. I'd taken a Propranolol an hour ago, washing the pill down with an espresso from the green room's coffee machine. The caffeine counteracted the anxiolytic effects of the beta-blocker, but I couldn't forgo my vice. Going without caffeine gave me wicked headaches. The irony, huh?

"You doin' okay?" came a low voice, audible over the sounds of production on the sidelines. *Brooke.*

"What do you mean?" I asked, trying to play it cool. Anxiety had to be telegraphed in each line of my posture.

Light blue eyes found me and infused me with a warmth that fueled my nerves rather than alleviating them. Ruby red lipstick adorned Brooke's famous pout—seen on theater screens and gracing the pages of *Seventeen*. "You seem a little nervous, that's all," Brooke said. Ridiculously white teeth peeked out from the crimson. "I still get nervous." Her mouth quirked upwards. "Not as much as I used to, though," she added.

"Yeah... a little. I've never been great at talking in front of people," I admitted.

Her eyebrow arched. "Don't they make you guys do oral boards? Like on *Grey's Anatomy*?"

I snapped my fingers. "I remember that episode! I forgot you were on it." A lie. I knew exactly when and where my teenage crushes popped up on the big or little screens. But she didn't need to know that.

Brooke theatrically tossed her blonde hair behind her shoulder and did a little bow. "Doctor #5 at your service."

My cheeks bloomed with heat. "Yeah... only certain specialties take oral boards. Not neurology. Thankfully. I would've probably died from fright."

"C'mon, you save lives, Dr. Absinthe," she said, waving her delicate wrist. "Talking to little ol' me in front of a camera? It's gonna be a cakewalk compared to the stuff you see every day." I hoped she was right. "Break a leg!" Brooke called out, making her way to her chair. She made it with seconds to spare.

"Let's go people!" someone shouted, and the din dimmed. Theme music played, and the studio audience cheered, clapping mostly on beat. I struggled to keep a neutral expression. Benign and bland. Professional. The last thing I needed to read tomorrow on Reddit was how everyone thought I looked like a massive bitch or—horror of all horrors—be made into a stupid meme.

Brooke blasted the camera with her megawatt smile, and I fought an overwhelming urge to fidget. Her co-host Drake followed suit, displaying teeth too perfect to be anything but veneers. Massive shoulders flexed in his tailored jacket, reminding me of The Hulk. "Welcome to *The Show!*" Brooke crooned.

The audience cheered.

Drake quickly added, "And boy, what a show we have for y'all today!"

"A real... double feature," Brooke said. "Like me back in the day!" She tossed her hair behind her shoulder again—a signature move apparently. The crowd tittered. At one time, Brooke was the reigning Teen Queen, starring in romantic comedies. She had minor roles in a few horror flicks; usually slashed to death in various stages of undress. She'd had two movies in the box office at the same time hence her double feature comment. In one she played a girl afflicted with a particularly cruel form of cancer and in the other; she was hacked into tiny bits by a maniacal Furby.

My little crush on Brooke Santori only compounded my social anxiety. *What the fuck was I thinking?* I should have taken *two* Propranolol. And a Xanax. Who knows? Maybe I'd drop dead before speaking, alleviating this whole disaster. If I were lucky.

Drake Alderstar laughed. "You're right about that, Brooke!" He turned his big frame and looked into the opposite camera. "Today, we have two guests who couldn't be more different."

"One is a doctor and the other—" Brooke started.

"—is a former pro basketball player!" Drake finished.

The crowd murmured excitedly.

"Dr. Aldea Absinthe!" Brooke called out. "She's a board-certified neurologist, who—in addition to being a total babe—" she shot me a smoldering look out of the corner of her eyes that sent my heart racing "—is pioneering migraine treatment! And dare we say? Nearing a cure?"

The crowd made the appropriate oohs and aahs and clapped.

I blushed. I couldn't believe they were clapping *for me*. If only Mom could see me now.

Drake Alderstar looked near tears; such was his excitement. "And our other guest: Shawn Gilbert!" Drake gushed.

Anything else Drake said was drowned out by the roar of the crowd. They stamped their feet and clapped their hands with unbridled enthusiasm, making my round of applause a wet noodle in comparison. Shawn was the real draw. I was the brains—and according to Brooke; the looks—while Shawn was the talent. Shawn thrust his arms up, basking in the ambiance.

Brooke and Drake waited for the applause to die. Once the crowd quieted, her blonde head swiveled and Brooke looked into my eyes, filling my veins with ice. "Dr. Absinthe, it's a *pleasure* to meet you,"

Just talk. Be normal. Easy peasy. "Thanks for having me, Brooke," I said.

Brooke's eyes sharpened. "Tell me about your work. About *you*."

Ignoring my hammering heart, I said, "That I can do, Brooke!" I looked into the camera and squared my shoulders. "I'm from Colorado, born and raised." The audience whooped as much as could be expected for Southern California. "I went to college in Colorado Springs. Medical school in Denver. Headed out to Oregon for my neurology residency." I pumped my fist in the air and added, "Go Ducks!" which elicited a few hoots from the audience.

"What brought you back to Colorado?" Brooke asked, cocking her head to the side.

"Work," I answered. "Work and... my mom."

"Did something happen?" Brooke asked in a soft voice.

I paused, taking a moment to swig water from the mug in front of me. It never got easier to talk about but—

"She got sick." Sick: a catch all term. Could be something as innocuous as the common cold or a pesky hemorrhoid. Or rampaging cancer. Autoimmune diseases. Fates worse than death—and of those, there were many. Paralysis with uncanny awareness, perfectly able to think and feel, unable to do a damn thing about it. Losing the ability to breathe on your own.

And my mom won the veritable lottery of suffering.

"What do you mean by *sick*?" Drake asked in a prissy tone that annoyed me.

Just breathe. I replied, "ALS." Would I have reacted the same way if Brooke asked? I thought not.

Drake's forehead wrinkled with supreme concentration that made him look constipated. "It has another name, right?" he asked in that smug *I-read-the-Wikipedia-entry-thirty-minutes-ago-and-now-I'm-an-expert* way that pissed me off.

"You're right. Lou Gehrig's disease—"

Drake cut in, "—named for the famous baseball player!" He glanced around the studio proudly and I half expected an intern to run out and slap a *Good Job* sticker on his broad chest.

"Yep," I agreed flatly.

"What exactly is... Lou Gehrig's disease?" Drake asked.

How to answer without scaring the living daylights out of everyone? I could tell him how the disease masqueraded as mere clumsiness in the beginning.

"Oops!" Mom would call out from the kitchen, voice punctuated by glass exploding in a thousand different directions, followed by a wet splatter against the linoleum. "Damn cup," she'd say, assigning blame to an inanimate object rather than herself. And who wouldn't? At least... the first few times. If she'd noticed anything—she kept it to herself. The injuries were minor: a sprained wrist, bruises from routinely smacking into furniture, stubbed toes. Until they weren't. I remembered her first ER visit and her swollen shut left eye, a fat purple plum juicy with stagnant blood: a hematoma.

"It's nothing, Aldea. I slept terribly last night. I'm tired. I was walking around half-asleep and fell. Shit happens," she said. The first whispers of disquiet stirred then but I kept them to myself. Not that it would have mattered anyway.

"It's a progressive disease," I said, answering Drake's insipid question. "It destroys your nerve cells. The ones responsible for movement, for breathing, and—" I faltered, remembering her last rattling exhalations. Brooke caught my eye and gave me an encouraging nod. Rather than increasing my nerves, a strange calm settled over me. Regaining my momentum, I continued, "—swallowing." It sounded like a dirty joke but that's when I realized the gravity of the issue: when my mother could no longer swallow.

I remembered the day everything changed with startling clarity. It always went like that, didn't it? The mind seemed uniquely conditioned to hold onto bad memories, hoarding them and examining them like a dragon nosing through its hoard of gold. Bad memories weren't shiny bits of beauty though—far from it. They were impossibly decayed with edges consumed by ragged rust. Painful. Sifting through such memories—no matter how delicately one sorted through them—always left wounds.

I'd been curled up on the couch with a book—nothing medical. Something fun. My mother's panicked voice immediately caught my attention and goosebumps raced up my forearms at its *off-ness*. Book tumbled from my lap, and I bolted to the kitchen. Tears streaked down her face and the front of her neck bobbed. Her mouth opened and what came out was wet and ragged. A croak, then a painful rasp. "Aldea... I can't... I can't swallow." Her eyes were wide with fear, her voice full of phlegm. Rivulets of drool poured from her mouth and a brown stain—coffee—soaked the front of her pajama shirt. She made another noise; that of a strangled animal. That broke my paralysis. With shaking fingers, I dialed 911, concerned about the time crunch already in place. A stroke: that's what I'd thought. Wrong.

It was *much worse.*

18

Rachel

I watched the monitor backstage. Aldea answered the questions Drake lobbed with poise, despite her confession earlier of: *I feel like puking my guts out.*

"Need a Zofran?" I asked, reaching into my purse. "I never go anywhere without it."

Nodding vigorously, she said, "Yes please! It'll pair well with my Propranolol."

"One of my nursing school classmates swore by that stuff before presentations," I said. "Not that I've ever tried it." I handed her the Zofran enclosed in foil and she peeled off the backing and placed the pill under her tongue. I couldn't blame her; the thought of speaking onstage made me nauseated too. The media expressed some interest in my and Shawn's relationship at the beginning, but we were relatively boring. They never resorted to paparazzi helicopters to snag a pic or reporters scaling fences. I'd been lucky to not have to contend with that kind of attention and couldn't imagine so many eyes staring all at once.

The audience laughed and I glanced down at the monitor again. Shawn sported a huge shit-eating grin after cracking a joke. Damn... he looked handsome in his new suit, fresh haircut, and neatly trimmed beard. My heart flipped, imaging him pulling me into his arms later.

"So, are you saying you're the Terminator now?" Drake asked.

Shawn chuckled. "Well, I do have a chip in my head but I'm pretty sure Dr. Absinthe didn't program me to kill John Connor or anything. But you never know."

Drake turned to Dr. Absinthe who answered with a charming shrug. Turning to the camera, Drake said with a wink, "Well, if and when it happens, you know we'll cover it!"

"Oh, I'm sure," Shawn answered. He leaned back in his chair and readjusted his cufflinks. "But seriously? Dr. Absinthe saved my life. Every day was hell. I lived with a constant headache, and I'd tried *everything*."

"Everything?" Brooke asked.

Shawn nodded. "*Everything*. Pills, supplements, shots, massage, Reiki." He counted on his fingers, looking up in deep concentration. "Chiropractors, neurologists, neurosurgeons, acupuncturists, faith healers—you name it, I saw them." And he had. Sometimes I worried what might have happened if we hadn't been together while he sought treatment. One doctor wrote him prescriptions for Soma and Percocet, telling him to pop them any time he had a headache—which was constantly. Had I not intervened, I wondered if he would've gotten hooked blindly following that dumb doctor's orders. I'd seen too many patients made into addicts due to chronic pain, sometimes even resorting to heroin when their doctors—the ones who created the monster in the first place—finally cut them off.

"How did you come across Dr. Absinthe?" Drake asked.

"A friend—Lewis Perry—got traded to Denver and settled down there. His wife gets terrible migraines and Dr. Absinthe treated her. He knew about my headaches, so he told me about her."

Brooke said, "I'm assuming Dr. Absinthe also cured his wife's migraines?"

Shawn's eyes crinkled. "Yup."

"Wrapping up, what parting words do you two have for our audience?" Drake said.

Dr. Absinthe smiled. "Thanks for having me, Brooke. Drake." Diamonds glinted on her earlobes. "If you're suffering from migraines—you don't have to. Get in touch for a free consultation and together we'll see if you are a candidate for Dr. Absinthe's Migraine Chip!"

The audience roared—giving *me* a bit of a headache. Their cheers petered out and a chorus of eyes stared expectantly at Shawn.

He said, "I'm not sponsored by Nike anymore, but I used to be so I'm gonna use their slogan: Just Do It. Don't wait. Fix your headaches today."

The audience laughed, and someone off stage yelled: "That's it, we're done!"

People jostled past me, busy worker bees, and I spotted Shawn. "Hey handsome!" I called out. Shawn rewarded me with a grin and gathered me in his arms for a hug. I inhaled deeply, smelling his cologne with hints of cedar and sandalwood along with the peppermint gum he always chewed. "You did great!" I added, "Looked great too."

"Thanks babe," Shawn murmured into my hair.

"What about me?" Shawn released me and we both looked at Dr. Absinthe. Her former bravado had gone, and she twisted her hands nervously.

"You did amazing too," I said.

Dr. Absinthe's tension melted. "Oh, thank God. I hated every second."

"Shall we all go out for a drink?" Shawn asked. "Celebrate?"

I'd been hoping for some one-on-one time but... "Sure babe," I answered.

"Count me in!" Dr. Absinthe said.

19

Dr. Absinthe

"How was your trip?" Taylor asked, tugging a red beanie over dark curls. She looked fabulous in scrubs covered in dog hair but in real clothing? Wowza. A form-fitting sweatshirt hugged her curves, topped with a puffy black vest. Spots of color dotted her cheeks and I swooned. Brooke Santori made me nervous in a starstruck crush sort of way, but Taylor was the real deal.

I licked my vanilla cone. Despite the cooler weather, I'd been craving it. One cone for me and a hot chocolate for Taylor. "It was good. I was nervous as hell before taping but once I started—" I shrugged. "It just flowed, I guess."

"Want to know a secret?"

I smiled. "Yeah."

Taylor leaned forward. "I already watched the episode, and you did amazing." Her gaze lingered on my lips. "Brooke paled in comparison to you, my dear," she said in a teasing tone, fully aware of my painful celebrity crush.

"Oh, stop it," I said, snaking my tongue out towards my ice cream. "She really did it for me in the movie with the Furby, you know."

"Doesn't she die first? In a very short mini skirt if I remember correctly."

I nodded. "I'll have you know: her mini skirt was an important item in my sexual awakening. *Attack of the Furby*. An absolutely campy, terrible movie. I loved every second of it."

"Did you do anything else fun there?" Taylor asked, lips pursing to take a sip of her hot chocolate.

"Dinner with Shawn and Rachel." . Steak tartare, Caesar salad with anchovies, and classic spaghetti for me. Two glasses of wine. Despite my exhaustion, I'd had a good time.

Except...

No. Don't think about it. I pushed the thought away.

Taylor said, "Shawn did well too." She was right: he had. He'd made a comeback, becoming a social media darling almost overnight. And as a result, business was booming. I was booked months out, everyone inquiring about the "Miracle Migraine Chips" as the media called them. I had to admit: it had a nice ring to it.

"What's his wife like?" Taylor asked.

"She's great. Very supportive. Actually—" I said, gesturing with my nibbled waffle cone. "I helped nab her a job in the ER. They always need nurses."

Taylor's eyes widened. "Shawn Gilbert married an ER nurse?"

"Yep. They met when he got injured. She took care of him."

"Wow," Taylor remarked. "That's very Nicholas Sparks, don't you think? Pro basketball player falls for Florence Nightingale reincarnated. He loses his memory but doesn't forget their love."

I butted in, "He didn't really lose his memory, he had headaches... remember?"

She flapped her hand. "It's more dramatic if he loses his memory. Haven't you seen *The Notebook*?"

"Of course, I've seen *The Notebook*. Rachel McAdams is in it." I used to watch the movie over and over as a teen—marinating in a weird mixture of hot-and-bothered and clinically depressed. I always sobbed my eyes out at the end. I couldn't help it; I was a romantic at heart.

"Are they super in love?" Taylor asked. "Like making out and stuff at the table?"

I playfully swatted at her shoulder. "Taylor, you are such a gossip!"

She batted her eyes. "I know, I know. But you love it."

"That's true," I replied, thinking back to dinner. To Shawn and Rachel. They held hands under the table and exchanged lingering glances. Still had that chemistry. "They adore each other," I replied. I wondered what it was like; being married like that. Sharing secrets, knowing your spouse's quirks and silly habits. But could someone ever truly know a person? Did anyone fully know anyone else?

I wondered if Rachel knew everything about Shawn. Somehow, I doubted it.

Taylor's eyebrows knitted together. "Everything okay?"

I considered lying, saying: totally! but the concerned expression on Taylor's face did me in. Plus... as my girlfriend—potentially my life partner—wasn't transparency the best option? "Not really," I answered, keeping my eyes trained on a man walking an adorable pug wearing a yellow vest.

Taylor grabbed my hand. "Tell me what's wrong." Her thumb rubbed reassuring circles on my palm.

"I'm worried... about the chip," I admitted.

She squeezed my hand. "What about it?"

"Well... there was an incident at dinner with Shawn."

A flock of birds swarmed overhead, drawing Taylor's attention momentarily away from me. She watched them settle on nearby powerlines before turning back to me. "Tell me what happened."

So, I told her:

"Gonna hit the little girls' room." Rachel excused herself from the table and sashayed in search of the restroom. A man at the bar ogled her ass with unabashed interest. In a cartoon world he'd be a wolf in a tuxedo with steam blowing out his ears.

"Fucking prick," Shawn hissed.

What? I jerked my head, shocked by the pure venom in his words. I'd never heard Shawn talk like that. "What?" I asked. Wrinkles creased his forehead and his dark eyes flashed—suddenly hard and flinty. His jaw muscle clenched. Unclenched. Nostrils flared. He looked like a raging bull gearing up to charge. All visages of *nice guy* dropped away in an instant. Oh shit.

"Hey, Shawn, listen…" I started. He looked seconds away from hurdling the table and leaping on the dude, taking him down like a cheetah would an unsuspecting gazelle. Shawn's breath hitched quickly, and a bead of sweat rolled down his temple. A faint twitch pulled his right eye upwards. "It's not a big deal." I held my hands up in front of me, trying to distract him, bring him back to the here-and-now. "Fuck that guy. He doesn't matter. He's not worth your time."

He cracked his knuckles—*pop, pop, pop,* miniature gunshots—and muttered, "I could fucking kill him with my bare hands. Looking at my wife like that. Can you fucking believe it?"

Whoa. Did he have a massive jealousy thing? Or an anger problem I didn't know about? "How about you don't? The accompanying press would torpedo everything to shit," I joked/not joked.

Something flickered across his face—there then gone—like a signal crackling through a synapse. Scowl became smile, and he replied, "Everything's fine, Aldea. Don't worry. Thanks." Every muscle in his body visibly relaxed.

"But—" I started, utterly confused by the rapid change in his mood.

"—What did I miss?" Rachel asked, flopping down into her chair.

I glanced at Shawn who grinned broadly at her. Like a switch flipped: irate to fine. "Just chatting about how cute you were," Shawn said, syrupy sweet—complete Jekyll-and-Hyde.

I offered a weak laugh and let the matter drop. The rest of dinner passed without incident. I ordered tiramisu to go and after returning to my room, showered, and changed into comfy pajamas; then slid under the covers with takeout box in hand. Forking creamy goodness into my mouth, I luxuriated in the distinct cinnamon and coffee flavor while running through the evening's events, circling back to the expression on Shawn's face. *And don't forget about Aubrey,* my mind whispered. She'd snapped too. Then there was Mrs. Combs... what if something caused the accident? Something I did?

My worries followed me to my subconscious, filling my dreams with anxiety that night and since. Was this merely a side of Shawn I'd never seen before? Macho, threatened Shawn or... what if the chip—

"Taylor, I really think there's a problem with the chip," I confided. "And I don't know what to do about it," I said. "I have to make this work. I *have* to."

"Listen, it'll be fine—" Taylor started.

I grabbed her arm. "—just listen." Taylor mutely nodded and I continued, "The chip already failed once; remember, it wasn't even designed for headaches—I'd meant it for ALS. For—" my voice cracked "—my Mom. I didn't want anyone else to go through what she went through, what we went through. I had such high hopes for it and when it fell flat... it nearly killed me. I moped around, called into work too often, drank too much—I felt like a huge loser, a failure." A rueful laugh escaped my lips. "Babe, it was a fucking accident I even figured out it worked for migraines! One of the ALS patients—while steadily declining from the disease—mentioned her migraines were gone... it was total luck I even connected the dots and figured it out."

"You're not giving yourself enough credit, Aldea. The fact is: you did figure it out. Period. And now you're helping people."

A sour taste filled my mouth. "But what if... I'm causing other problems?" Before I could stop myself, I spilled my concerns about Aubrey. Two patients could be a coincidence but... I wasn't sure about that.

She gave me a reassuring smile. "Don't worry, babe. We'll tackle this, together."

Her words eased my fears some, but anxiety still simmered in my stomach. The stakes were even higher than before. I had a former professional athlete singing my praises and people were listening. Hell, they'd even mentioned me on a few nighttime talk shows—and not even as the punchline of some shitty joke. But that could change on a dime; if something was wrong, if something truly horrible happened... it was my livelihood at risk, my reputation, my ego, not to mention whatever toll it took on the affected patients.

And if this didn't succeed—it'd be like failing my mother all over again. If the chip wouldn't work with ALS...

It had to work.

It had to.

20

Dr. Absinthe

DESPITE MY BETTER JUDGMENT I dialed Dr. Chase's number. I couldn't stop picturing Aubrey pummeling an elderly lady to a pulp, her tortoiseshell glasses flying into the air. My mind kept circling back to the chip. That damn chip.

"Hello?" came Dr. Chase's prim answer.

Dr. Chase! It's Dr. Absinthe."

Silence.

"Who?"

Not this shit again. "Dr. Absinthe. Neurology. We talked last week about Aubrey—"

He snorted. "Dr. Absinthe! That's right. What might I do for you this fine day, my dear?"

Puke. "Oh... I was just checking in on Aubrey. How's she doing?"

He made a clucking noise with his tongue. "Not well, I'm afraid. She's been... impulsive."

"Impulsive?" I repeated.

"Impulsive. She attacked her roommate—a very nice lady with a persistent delusion that she is Sacajawea, you know, the Native American woman who aided Lewis and Clark—because she wouldn't give Aubrey her chocolate pudding."

Typical psychiatrist, dropping American History tidbits into casual conversation. I fought the urge to laugh. "Uh, sure."

"Very disappointing. I've placed her in isolation for the time being and I'm trialing some new meds."

"I see. Would you mind if I came and saw her?" I asked. "Just to check a few things out. Make sure this isn't a neurological issue," I hastily added.

"Be my guest. But don't get too close. We caught her throwing feces the other day—she nearly hit one of the med students."

Later, one of my patients no showed. I returned to the psych unit and a burly orderly escorted me to Aubrey's room. He unlocked the door and motioned for me to go inside.

"Thanks," I said.

He nodded. "I'll be right out here. Holler if you need anything."

"Will do."

The door shut behind me. I peered at Aubrey and recoiled. She looked like absolute hell. Her blonde hair was matted, sorely in need of a wash and a brushing. Maybe even a shearing. Dark circles rimmed her eyes and her normally golden skin had a sallow appearance. The tan paper scrubs hung off her frame, revealing prominent collarbones.

I cleared my throat. "Uh, hey Aubrey?"

Sluggishly she inclined her head. Dazed eyes stared into mine and then sharpened. "Dr. Absinthe? Is that you?" she slowly said, obviously under the influence of some sort of sedative or anti-psychotic.

I smiled. "It is me. Dr. Chase told me you were in here and I wanted to check in on you. See how you were holding up." I glanced around her woefully bare room and inwardly cringed.

A hoarse giggle escaped her chapped lips. "Not very fucking well I'm afraid, Dr. Absinthe. I don't know if you heard but I'm in the fucking loony bin."

"I... see that," I replied.

A few tears plopped to the padded floor. "It's not my fault," Aubrey said forlornly.

"No?" I asked.

She jumped up—and I involuntarily took a few steps back, unnerved by how quickly she moved—and pounded her fists on the padded wall. "No!" *Pound.* "It's not!" *Pound.* "I can't." *Pound.* "Help it." *Pound.* I meanly thought: Queen's, *We Will Rock You* (*Psych Ward Remix*).

"You can't help it?" I repeated. "What do you mean by that?" All the tone went out of her body, and she collapsed into a heap and dissolved into sobs. "It's okay, Aubrey. You can tell me. I'm here to help," I said in my best talking-to-animals-and-sick-people voice.

She cried until her breath hitched. Once her tears petered out, she looked up at me again. "That's just it. I can't help it. I get mad and it's like I lose control." She uncurled her fingers from tight fists. "Like at the grocery store? That old lady pissed me off but lots of things piss me off, right? We all have those thoughts: *what if I punched that guy that cut in line?* or whatever? It was like that, I had that thought and before I could even think, I was on top of her, hitting her. I couldn't stop myself." I ran my fingers along my closed laptop but said nothing. Aubrey continued, "Even now, I can't stop myself. I got mad at my roommate, and I slapped the shit out of her. I can't control my emotions. I cry at the drop of a hat. I'm not myself. Something is wrong with me!" Tears tracked down her face and she gave me a haunted look. "You believe me, don't you?"

I did. I did. "I believe you, Aubrey. Now... if I could possibly help you, would you want that?"

She frantically nodded her head. "Yes, yes! Anything! Please. Anything!"

I opened my laptop. "I'd like to tinker with your migraine chip; make sure that's not the problem. Is that okay?"

Fear flashed across her face. "Will my migraines come back?"

"I don't know," I admitted. "Maybe."

"Because if they come back... I don't know what I'll do. I can't live like that either, Dr. Absinthe."

I shrugged. "Listen... in medicine, nothing is ever 100%. The migraines might come back but—"

"Then I don't want it!" Aubrey screamed.

I took a step back. "You don't want me to—"

"No! Get out! GET OUT!" Aubrey's voice rose sharply and fearing what might follow, I did just that: I got the hell out. Someone capable of beating the tar out of an elderly woman wasn't someone I needed to trifle with. If someone wasn't in their right mind and didn't have to capacity to truly understand what was at stake here; if that certain someone was currently in isolation in a psych ward—did I really need her permission to try to fix this?

No, I decided. Sometimes doctors knew what was best for their patients and I had to do something. Try something. I had an ethical obligation really.

21

Dr. Absinthe

S TILL CLUTCHING MY LAPTOP, I walked through the reception area's door and immediately was greeted by a fucking disaster.

"Listen lady, you need to get out of my face and sit down. NOW!" Billie bellowed, eyes flashing. The lady in question: Mrs. Dora Sale, a 40-year-old woman who admittedly, wasn't my favorite patient—far from it. Dora had a nasty habit of faking seizures to score benzodiazepines and unfortunately, was well known at local hospitals for her exploits. Her malingering was complicated by an actual epilepsy diagnosis and the fact that Dora faked seizures with the acting prowess of Meryl Streep—foaming at the mouth, pissing her pants, and feigning unresponsiveness like an absolute pro. Surprisingly, she'd shown up for her afternoon appointment—bad news for me since one more no show meant I could fire her as a patient and never have to see her again.

Dora crossed her arms over her ample chest. "I ain't sittin' down 'til someone gets me some Ativan. I feel a seizure comin' on." An ugly sneer twisted her lips.

"I told you, *that* is not happening. Now sit down and shut up." Billie hissed, barely audible from my vantage point near the door.

As incensed as she was, Billie didn't even notice me standing there. Two patients in the waiting room avidly observed the situation.

Dora retorted, "Guess I'll just have a seizure and DIE then!" Theatrically she put the back of her hand against her forehead—channeling Scarlett O'Hara about to swoon—and her shoulders started slumping forward.

"Oh no you don't!" Billie cried out. She was out of her chair in a flash and vaulted the reception desk with the finesse of an Olympian and—before I could even think, let alone react—had gripped Dora's shoulders so tightly her knuckles blanched.

My mouth dropped open. Was this really happening?

"Let me go!" Dora shrieked, all pretense of her "seizure" abandoned by the unexpected assault.

Billie sneered. "I thought you were having a *seizure*," she said in a singsong voice. "Quite the recovery you made. A miracle really." The tips of her fingers disappeared into Dora's pudge and an animalistic snarl overtook her face.

"You're hurtin' me!" Dora cried out and the fear in her voice broke my paralysis.

I surged forward, getting between my patient and an irate Billie. "Whoa, whoa, whoa. Let's just calm down, now," I said, pushing Billie away from Dora. A thunderous scowl twisted Billie's features and her eyes narrowed. Her stare was cold without an ounce of recognition, only pure fury. She took a step towards me, her fists clenched. "Billie!" I said, taking an involuntary step back. "Billie, listen to me!" Both hands instinctively went in front of me, palms out. She continued to advance. Nostrils flared.

"What's going on here?" Claire's voice boomed from behind the reception desk. "What the—"

Seeing the standoff taking place in the waiting room, Claire hustled through the door, placing herself on my right side. Billie's eyes flicked to Claire and something within her faltered, whether it was her lizard brain calculating the new odds with the addition of Claire or some semblance of sanity, and she stopped coming at me. All visages of rage fell away and for a moment, she looked utterly blank, devoid of any sort of emotion. The rapid switch and resultant *nothing* unnerved me more than the anger.

"Billie, what the hell?" Claire cried out.

"I'm gettin' the fuck out of here!" Dora screamed, moving remarkably quick for someone who'd been about to seize moments earlier. Before the door closed behind her, she pointed and yelled, "And I ain't comin' back to this shithole. Not with that—that—crazy bitch!" Thank God for small favors. Hopefully she didn't press charges.

"C'mon," Claire muttered, grasping Billie's hand, and tugging her through the door that led to the back. "Let's go to the breakroom." Billie followed, meek as a lamb.

I turned to the two patients in the waiting room and put on my best customer service smile. "Sorry about that. Someone will be with you shortly." Not waiting for their responses, I met Claire and Billie in the breakroom. A bottle of water sat in front of Billie—capped and untouched. Billie glowered at it. I took a seat across from her and took in her wan appearance. Makeup was smeared across her eyelids as if she'd gone to sleep without removing it and a smattering of zits decorated her chin and cheeks, some capped with whiteheads. Her cheekbones looked sharper than they used to and gazing down, I realized her shirt hung on her. She looked like hell.

"Billie," I started, keeping my voice low and calm although all I wanted to say was: *what the fuck was that?* "What's going on?"

She kept her gaze on her ragged cuticles. "Nothin'," Billie muttered sullenly.

"Bullshit nothing," Claire said. "What's going on with you?" She stared at Billie, hands on her hips.

"Listen, Billie, I'm not mad but you need to tell us what's going on," I said. I was more freaked out than mad.

Billie's face crumpled inwards, and she started crying.

"Oh Billie," Claire said, putting her hands on Billie's shoulders. "It's okay, hon. It's okay," she murmured in her best mom voice—the exact same voice my mom used when I came in with a scraped knee and tears.

The sobbing ebbed, petering out to mere sniffles. Billie looked up, meeting my eyes. She looked so... tired. It reminded me of looking in the mirror in residency during a grueling call shift, utterly hopeless and exhausted. "Everything's going to shit," Billie said. Claire squeezed her shoulder reassuringly. "And that bitch just... she just sent me over the edge. I'm sorry."

"Believe me Billie, I've fantasized about strangling her too but... you can't be doing that, no matter what's going on in your life, okay?" I replied. She weakly nodded. "Is there anything I can do you for?" I asked. "If you need to talk or if something's bothering you—"

Billie quickly cut in, "I'm fine. It's fine. I lost control for a second. It won't happen again."

"No, it *won't* happen again," I said. "I'll cut you some slack this time but never again. Now, take the rest of the day off. Get some rest. You look exhausted."

She gave me an anemic, thin-lipped smile. "Okay. Thanks Dr. Absinthe. I'm sorry. It *won't* happen again, I promise."

Billie hugged Claire and gathered her things from her cubby. "See you guys tomorrow. Tomorrow will be better." She left.

Claire and I stared at each other.

"I missed the beginning of all that," Claire said. "What the hell happened?"

I shook my head. "I don't know. When I came in, they were arguing. Sounds like Dora was demanding Ativan, per usual, and Billie snapped. Jumped the desk and grabbed Dora. If I hadn't jumped in, she probably would have beat the shit out of her." I stopped, remembering the cold look in her eyes and how she advanced toward me, ready to vent her ire on someone else, anyone else. I'd felt... afraid.

Claire sighed. "I knew she was having some issues but this... this is bad."

"What issues?" I asked.

"Well... her boyfriend broke up with her. Slapped a restraining order on her from what I understand. Said that Billie was stalking him, threatening him. I know she's not sleeping. She barely eats. I figured she was a bit depressed—and who wouldn't be?"

"Yeah," I replied absently. I thought back to what Billie said:

I lost control for a second.

Then, I thought of Aubrey, what she'd told me:

I can't help it. I get mad and it's like I lose control of myself.

A chill skittered down my spine. I got to my feet. "Welp, better get back to work huh? If the patients in the waiting room didn't run out screaming, that is."

Claire chuckled. "Please, that's probably the most excitement they've had in years. It'll give 'em a great story to tell at dinner tonight."

"I'm gonna run to my office real quick, then I'll see the first patient, okay?"

"You got it boss."

I collected my laptop, shut the door, and opened the chip program. I scrolled down to Aubrey's name and studied her settings. Inhibition seemed appropriate; not even turned up to its max potential. But... if the chip was somehow inhibiting impulse control, it stood to reason that decreasing the inhibition might resolve the problem—assuming the chip was even the issue. I wasn't completely convinced but Billie and Aubrey's words kept rattling around my mind:

I lost control.

I dialed Aubrey's settings back and slapped the laptop shut.

We'd see.

22

Rachel

T HE DAY WAS PAR for the course.

Crushing chest pressure, abdominal pains—most of which arrived with *Flamin' Hot Cheetos* in hand—along with various other maladies. Plenty of lacerations, weird rashes, and—as always—drug seekers jonesing for their next fix. I glanced at my watch. 4:05 p.m. Only three hours to go. I breathed a sigh of relief. Almost there.

"WE NEED HELP IN HERE!" boomed from Room 1; the room nearest the waiting room. The tone was one I'd had heard countless times before. The words weren't tinged by hysteria but had an unmistakable undercurrent of haste implied within. It meant: "*Shit is going down, everyone get your ass in here, NOW!*"

"Of course, right when I'm about to take a bathroom break," I muttered, grabbing my stethoscope and trauma sheers. I leapt up and rushed to Room 1, finding a mass of people surrounding the stretcher—mostly lookie-loos getting in the way of medical professionals. I elbowed my way through the throng of people, earning a curt *hey* which I ignored. On seeing the patient, I thought, *oh shit* but kept my expression professionally bland;

a carefully cultivated skill after seeing unimaginable horrors during my career.

He looked terrible. Sweaty and ashen faced; skin the color of dirty dishwater. His limbs jerked erratically like a downed live-wire after a thunderstorm and as I watched, he spewed a fountain of bloody vomit from his mouth, spraying the nearest lookie-loo who turned tail and fled the room with a disgusted scream closely followed by violent retching. All lookie-loos vacated the premises after that. Vomit had an uncanny way of clearing a room.

A tech checked the man's blood sugar, announcing: "145" to the room.

"What's going on?" I asked, leaping into action. I grasped the man's quivering arm firmly and started an IV on the first stick, then funneled blood into a rainbow of tubes.

From the head of the bed, Dr. Black answered: "Fuck if I know. Family dropped him off and he started seizing in triage. Went unresponsive." Dr. Black turned to me. "Rachel, draw up 2 milligrams of Ativan and grab the RSI box. This guy needs an airway, especially since he's doing his best Old Faithful impersonation." She readied her intubation supplies, bending the ET tube until it resembled a hockey stick, attaching a 10-cc syringe to the pilot balloon, inflating the cuff located at the tube's tip—ensuring there was no leak.

Everyone else jumped into action. Quick hands hooked the man to the cardiac monitor. Someone hauled the massive red crash cart to the bedside and slapped sticky patches on the man's sweaty chest—just in case. Another RN, Steve, handed me the Ativan vial and I drew up 2 mg and pushed it through the IV, chasing it with a saline flush.

His shaking abruptly ceased. One small victory. Then he went completely apneic.

"Shit! Guess I won't be needing those RSI meds after all," Dr. Black remarked. She sounded calm, almost bored. I doubted her heart rate spiked over 50 despite all the excitement. Dr. Black was one cool cucumber. The only time I recalled seeing her riled up was when snot from a trach patient rocketed into her hair. She took her position at the head of the bed and with fluid motions, Dr. Black intubated the man, sliding plastic through his vocal cords without issue. A respiratory therapist hooked the ET tubing to a ventilator, completing the ritual.

Airway now secured; Dr. Black turned to an anxious woman standing in the corner of the room who looked one breath from fainting dead away. Her dark eyes were haunted, a thousand-yard stare. Shock; I'd seen it a thousand times. Two spots of blush marked pale cheeks, and I spied a blot of purple peering out, an unmistakable marking: come tomorrow, she'd be sporting a nice shiner. Someone sat a chair next to the frazzled woman and—with a weary expression—she flopped down heavily.

"What happened?" Dr. Black asked, placing a comforting hand on the woman's shoulder.

The woman looked up with red-rimmed eyes and wrung her hands. Her wedding ring winked on her left hand, catching the overhead light. His wife I guessed. "He—we... were at home relaxing. He got a call from the office. Bad news—I guess—based on how he reacted. I don't know." She fidgeted. "He always had a temper but... he lost it. Started smashing things, grabbed a paperweight and hurled it."

Unconsciously, she stroked the blooming bruise on her cheek. "Then... he got a blank look on his face and—" her voice hitched and broke. Fat tears rolled down her cheeks. She gave a gusty sniffle and swiped her eyes. "He collapsed and started shaking. I don't know for how long... but it felt like eternity." She paused and shut her eyes. "Then he came to and was very confused. But I was able to get him up and out to the car. I brought him here straight away. Then—this happened." She spread her arms as if showcasing a prize on a game show but instead of gleaming appliances—bloody vomit and medical supplies were strewn about the room.

Dr. Black fired questions at the wife, barely taking a breath: "Any medical problems? Medications? Allergies? Surgeries? Anything different about today? Any drug use?"

The woman shook her head and noisily blew into a Kleenex she'd extracted from the depths of her purse. Lint clung to the edges. "No, he's healthy. No allergies. He used to be on Amitriptyline for his headaches, but he's been off that ever since Dr. Absinthe inserted the migraine chip." She stared at the ceiling and her brow creased. "Oh. He had his appendix out as a kid. Everything today was fine other than him complaining he felt tired. I know he had a hard week at work." She shrugged, adding, "He's a day trader. His job is *very* stressful."

A migraine chip? Like Shawn's?

"When did he get that chip put in?" I asked.

The wife sniffled. "A few months ago. Stress induced headaches. You know—his job. He hasn't had a single headache since she put the chip in." Her face brightened. "Can you please call Dr. Absinthe and let her know he's here? She's amazing."

"Of course," I answered, earning a sidelong look from Dr. Black. It was surely a coincidence—loads of people suffered from headaches and I'd seen more and more patients with the chip. I hadn't seen any adverse effects from it. At least, not yet. And who knew if this even had *anything* to do with the chip.

Still... a seed of doubt wormed its way into my gut and my stomach churned. What if there *were* issues with the chip? They weren't FDA-approved. A horrible image filled my mind: me sitting wearily at Shawn's bedside while a ventilator kept him alive. Countless drips infusing. Alarms braying. An *unfortunate complication,* Dr. Absinthe would say. *I had no idea.*

Within the hour, Dr. Absinthe breezed into the ER, wearing a perfectly tailored white coat. Dr. Absinthe greeted me at the nurses' station. "Rachel! Fancy meeting you here. How's Shawn doing?"

"Fine," I answered.

"Good! Thanks for giving me a call and letting me know about Mr. Reynolds." Dr. Absinthe exclaimed, her eyes glittering. "Now, where's my patient?"

I pointed to Room 1. The drapes were open, and all was calm after the initial flurry of activity. The only noises were the ventilator delivering a breath every five seconds and quiet sniffles from the patient's wife periodically.

"Thank you." Dr. Absinthe turned towards the room and strode off. Her hair and coat fluttered like she was Marilyn Monroe standing over the sewer grate in her iconic pose. *Gorgeous people created their own wind,* I figured. All the better to walk around like a goddess. She left a rich perfume in her wake. Chanel No. 5. My mother swore by it, hoarding it like a doomsday prepper with canned goods. I'd recognize it anywhere.

Ten minutes passed and Dr. Absinthe reappeared at the nurses' station where she found me charting—a never-ending task. "Rachel? I don't know where Dr. Black is, but can you tell her to put the admission orders under me? I'll take him primarily."

I gaped. "Wait... *you're* taking him primarily? He's gotta go to the ICU since he's tubed. I figured the intensivist would—" I trailed off. What in the world was going on here? It took an act of God to even get a neurologist to step foot in the ER and they certainly didn't admit patients primarily. Let alone critically ill, intubated patients! Something was *not* right here. Not right at all.

"Rachel. I'm perfectly capable of managing this patient on my own. I went to medical school and residency just like the ICU doc did, you know. Any monkey can manage a ventilator anyway." Her tone was haughty, but her face remained blandly pleasant.

"Yeah, but—" I started.

"Just tell Dr. Black. Thank you," Dr. Absinthe said, cutting me off. Discussion over.

23

Dr. Absinthe

Leaving the Emergency Department, I bolted to my office.

Billie glanced up as I hurried by. "Hey, Dr. Absinthe, Dr. Chase called for you. He wants you to call him back when you get a sec."

I groaned. "Ugh, fine. He's making this quite the habit."

Billie rubbed her eyes. She still looked tired as hell but seemed more herself today. "I know. He's weird."

"Tell me about it," I muttered as I walked off. What a fucking day. A sick ass patient in the ER and now Dr. Chase wanted to bother me. He could wait. The second my butt hit the chair, I pulled up Mr. Reynolds' head CT and scrolled through it. The cerebrum looked fine. But as I scrolled down, the brainstem popped into view and bright white hemorrhages filled the screen. Shit. Continuing through, I came across my chip—a faint density implanted at the level of the occiput. Not really near the area of hemorrhage but... I couldn't say for sure it hadn't contributed to Mr. Reynolds' ailment. Something like this—a bad outcome befalling a family man in the prime of his life—could torpedo my prospects right in the shitter.

What cures migraines? Brain bleeds!

Fuck. And the way Rachel looked at me; like she didn't quite trust me, skeptical as hell. I'd tried to act cool and non-bothered, like it was the most routine thing in the world for me to admit him. During residency, the neurology service often admitted their own patients, provided they weren't a total medical nightmare otherwise. But nowadays? No way. I hadn't admitted a patient in years! Sighing, I pulled up the day's call list. ICU: Dr. Denis. Finally, some good news. Dr. Denis and I had gone to residency together. Went out for drinks a few times. He'd expressed interest but since I batted for the other team, our relationship was strictly platonic. Not that he didn't harass me at every turn, but it was all good natured.

Picking up my office phone, I rang his personal cell. He answered after two rings. "Aldea! To what do I owe the pleasure? Want to go out and pick up some ladies?" he joked. "You know I'm a hell of a wing man." I could almost see him waggling his eyebrows.

Despite my nerves, I chuckled. "You wish. I'm actually dating someone—believe it or not."

"Oooooo Aldea! Who's the lucky lady?"

I grinned. "Spooky's veterinarian. Gotta thank the little shit for breaking his leg, I guess."

"I bet she's a real... pussy expert." Even through the phone I heard Don's lecherous grin.

"Ew, don't be gross," I admonished him, knowing it fell on deaf ears. "Hey—I need a favor from you."

A blast of cheering filled the phone and Don cursed. "Fucking Buffalos couldn't get a first down if their lives depended on it. Might as well put Ralphie in a damn jersey at this rate," he grumbled. "What do you need, Aldea?"

"I'm admitting a patient, Mr. Reynolds. Had status epilepticus and has a nasty bleed in the cerebellum." I paused. "I don't know what happened first. Seizure then bleed, or if the bleed caused the seizure. Anyway, he's intubated, and I need help managing the vent." I might have told Rachel a simple-minded primate could manage a vent, but I was totally full of shit.

Don whistled. "Look at the overachiever, actually admitting a patient yourself!"

"Yeah," I said, reluctant to say more. I had to figure out what the fuck had happened and didn't need other people mucking around in my business. Mrs. Reynolds told me about his preceding outburst in hitching sobs: *Like a switch flipped. Dr. Jekyll and Mr. Hyde.* What she described seemed almost like a psychotic break, buckling under the stress of a demanding job. One phone call and the house of cards fell apart. *He never hit me before,* she sobbed. *Never, ever. He just lost control.*

Lost control. Just like Aubrey. Like Billie. Like Shawn. Too many coincidences... if they were coincidences. I was really starting to wonder.

"Sure, I'll manage your vent. Easiest consult of the day." He lowered his voice. "The respiratory therapists are the ones that do everything. I just bark out orders and pontificate about vent settings like it fucking matters. Put the consult order in and feel free to call me if you need any help... or if you want to go out for drinks. I could use some lesbian mojo."

"You've got yourself a deal. Maybe I'll see if Taylor has any straight friends?"

Don whooped. "Give me someone who takes care of farm animals... I've got a cock they'd love to meet."

"You're a real class act, Don."

He chortled. "Don't I know it, babe." Without further ado, he hung up. Probably off to peruse PornHub... especially if the CU Buffalos weren't performing up to snuff.

I put the consult order in and turned back to the images of Mr. Reynolds' ruined brain. Significant edema had already set in and the on-call neurosurgeon, Dr. Jann, took one look at the scan and tactfully told me, "Mr. Reynolds here is totally fucked." I'd expected as much. There was a fine line of dealing with posterior circulation bleeds. Either you did nothing because it wasn't so bad; you had to intervene before it got too bad; or it was so bad you couldn't do shit about it. This clearly belonged to the third category. Sure, sometimes you had the odd medical miracle where a patient pulled through against all odds but—most likely—Mr. Reynolds was done for. Might be able to donate a few organs. Lord knows there were a ton of folks who needed new hearts, kidneys, and the like.

I sighed and despite wanting nothing more than to ignore Billie's message about Dr. Chase, I picked up the phone again and called.

"Yes?" Dr. Chase answered.

I gnashed my jaw. "Dr. Chase, it's Dr. Absinthe." I paused, waiting for him to say: *who?* like we hadn't talked several times recently.

"Aldea!" he said, surprising me. "Thanks for calling me back. I have terrible news I'm afraid." Of course, he had bad news. It was the day for it.

"What?" I asked flatly.

"It's Aubrey. She... well... she's dead."

"WHAT?" I roared. My stomach twisted. "What happened?" Dread filled me. Please let it be something totally unrelated; a heart attack, sepsis, anything.

"It's hard to say... yesterday evening we heard screaming from her room and by the time the orderlies and nurses got there—it was too late."

"What do you *think* happened?" I asked through gritted teeth.

"Well... I did review the camera footage—we have cameras in all the rooms—and it looked like she snapped. Started beating her head against the wall. My God it was a mess! Blood everywhere. They started CPR on her but... it was already too late." I could have told them CPR wasn't going to do shit if your brain was fucked.

"I'm sorry to hear that," I said. Cold coursed through my body and I felt oddly numb, distant from myself. "Will there be an autopsy?" I asked.

"Given the circumstances of her death, yes. I believe she'll be a coroner's case."

I pinched the bridge of my nose. "Will you let me know when you get the results?"

"Of course."

Hanging up, I realized my hands were shaking.

This was NOT good.

24

Shawn

"C'MON," I MUTTERED, TAPPING my fingers against the steering wheel.

I'd been in a standstill for the last ten minutes with no signs of progress. A simple trip to the store was turning into quite the ordeal. Hopefully the popsicles weathered the storm... and kept the eggs cool. Rachel had a bit of a sweet tooth, and I couldn't resist tossing a box of Bombsicles in the cart. While Aldea and I were in LA for the next round of appearances, she could binge Netflix and indulge in frozen processed sugar.

Horns bleated from up ahead, adding a back beat to the *Top Hits* radio pouring from the speakers. The Range Rover ahead of me crawled forward a foot—quite the progress. Not even worth pushing the gas pedal down.

SMASH!

My body jerked and the seatbelt cinched tightly. My teeth clamped shut and I bit my tongue, salty copper flavoring my taste buds. Faintly, I heard glass tinkle to the pavement—drowned out by Justin Bieber's crooning—and everything stilled, deadly silent despite the chorus of noise earlier.

Two things happened: dimly I thought, *someone just hit me.* Then a dangerous heat filled me, and my temper flared. *Fucking son-of-a-bitch.*

I shucked my seatbelt, threw the door open and leapt out. *Nikes* slapped on pavement, and I cut to the left—an echo of my glory days—my eyes peeled for the motherfucker who hit my car, rear-ending me in standstill traffic. Hot anger gripped my chest. My heart raced and my breathing quickened.

The bastard leapt from a lifted truck now sporting a crumpled hood. He wore scuffed cowboy boots, Wranglers, and a faded t-shirt displaying an ignorant Trump quote. Spotting me heading his way, his eyes widened, and mouth dropped open where two yellow teeth vied for dominance. "Hey now, hey! We don't need to go off half-cocked!" he said, taking a few steps back, his arms and hands extended in the hold-your-horses gesture.

I yelled, "Easy for you to say, asshole! *You're* the one that rear-ended *me!*"

On hearing *asshole*, his chest puffed up and his fists clenched. His muddy eyes narrowed. Sharpened. "The fuck you call me—you motherfucking piece of shit?" he spat.

Searing poison spread through me. "You're a redneck piece of shit!" Rage reddened my vision and my heartbeat thudded in my ears—fast and hard. I was only a few feet away from him—at my full height of 6'5" which was mediocre in the NBA but large in real life—and his expression pinched into one of: *Oh shit. I really, really fucked up.* Now, only inches away, I towered over the little prick. "You mind saying that to me again, asshole?" I hissed, "I wasn't sure I heard you right."

I expected him to deflate—right there in my shadow. *Sorry sir, I didn't say nothin'. Wanna exchange insurances, lickety-split? No harm, no foul.* All pussycat eyes and displaying his belly in surrender like a defeated dog. Fully anticipating this course of action, I felt my ire downshift.

Wrong again.

A mean sneer cut his face and tobacco juice dribbled down his chin. He drew himself up to his full height—maybe 5'5" with cowboy boots. "Lord knows how you didn't hear me, but I said: *you motherfucking piece of shit.*" He capped the statement off by hocking his chew on my shoes.

SPLAT!

Something within me broke, like a dam giving way and absolute fury gripped me. Distantly, I felt my right fist ball up and my feet shifted into a fighting stance—years of dealing with schoolyard bullshit roaring back. Every slight, insult, and deep-rooted pain I'd experienced fueled my temper's furnace—shoveling coal into billowing flames, stoking them ever higher. A rapturous sort of indignity flooded me, and I leapt forward, fist aimed at the redneck fuck's face.

Knuckles met flesh; there was a *crack* and the feeling of cartilage giving way.

Then my vision went black, and I remembered no more.

25

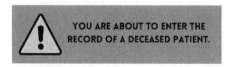

Rachel

After running my ass off all day, I snagged a moment of time between charting and acting as an RN—which some people seemed to think stood for *Refreshments and Narcotics* instead of Registered Nurse. Family members accosted me for cups of coffee (with *Stevia*, not sugar!) as I ran meds to a critical patient's room—then indignantly replied in a huff: *well, we're important too!* Stretching my arms above my head—enjoying the pull in my tight shoulders—I turned back to the computer.

Should I? Shouldn't I? I warred internally but as they said: *curiosity killed the cat. And satisfaction brought him back,* I reminded myself.

Badging into the computer, I was rewarded with a *beep* and the EMR popped up. At the top, I selected the *Recent Patients* tab and scrolled down. There. Mr. Reynolds. I clicked on his name and was rewarded with red block letters:

> ⚠ **YOU ARE ABOUT TO ENTER THE RECORD OF A DECEASED PATIENT.**

My heart sunk.

The EMR asked: *Continue?*

I had to know. I selected YES and waded through the auto-populated bullshit pervading the medical record. As far as nursing went, I qualified as one of the "babies," having never dealt with paper charting or T-sheets. The old-timers loved nothing more than to bitch about the extraneous detail added by the EMR and I had to admit they had a point. After scrolling through several pages documenting I's & O's, PT and OT notes which—predictably—were lacking since Mr. Reynolds was intubated and sedated, not quite up for wheeled walker treks up and down the hallway. And since he was dead... he'd never get that PT or OT consult.

I scrolled further and finally, hit pay dirt.

No more seizures as evidenced by the bedside EEG monitor but Dr. Absinthe who—in addition to her migraine chip exploits—apparently read EEGs commented: *complete electrocerebral activity x thirty minutes indicating brain death*. In a separate note, Dr. Absinthe detailed Mr. Reynolds' woeful lack of brainstem reflexes, laying it on thick regarding his prognosis which was labeled as *dismal: It is clear Mr. Reynolds has suffered brain death due to significant hypoxia. His CT scan—in addition to displaying a massive intracerebellar bleed that unfortunately is non-operative per Neurosurgery recs—shows clear indicators of hypoxic brain injury. He displays no meaningful reflexes, even after sedation was weaned. After extensive discussion with patient's wife—who acts as POA—decision was made to withdraw care. Donor Alliance contacted as patient is an organ donor.*

Wait. Something seemed off.

I quickly reviewed the chart, searching for another neurologist's note and after my third pass, had to admit defeat. No corroborating neurology note agreeing with Dr. Absinthe's diagnosis of brain death. As an ER nurse, I wasn't particularly versed in the cares that took place on med/surg or the ICU—especially since my clinicals in each were filled with giving bed baths, passing meds under strict supervision, and crying in the stairwell—but it was hospital policy to have two independent neurologists examine a potentially brain-dead patient. Fucking that up was a big no-no, akin to euthanizing someone that could have—in theory anyway—recovered. As I turned over this conundrum over in my mind, my cellphone buzzed and skittered across the nurses' station. I caught it before it tumbled to the germ-infested ground and glanced at the screen: Denver Police Department

What? With a shaking finger, I tapped accept. "Hello?" I said, struggling for calm and collected but panic bled into the greeting.

Angry shouting echoed in the background. "Hey, babe."

"Shawn! What's the matter? Are you okay? What happened?" The questions tumbled rapid fire from my mouth and my heart raced. I handled critical situations all day every day but when something involved me or my family, my nurse brain overloaded, and I tended towards near-mental breakdown.

"I'm fine. Don't get your panties in a bunch," he replied.

I gritted my teeth at his nonchalant attitude. "Then why the *fuck* are you calling me from what I'm assuming is the Denver Police Station based on my caller ID?" Some of my fear receded, replaced by annoyance.

He paused and without seeing him, I knew he'd shrugged. "My phone broke."

"Okay... but that still doesn't explain the whole Police Station thing," I said. Sometimes Shawn infuriated me by never providing the full information. I had to pull it out of him like an ingrown toenail embedded in tender skin.

Shawn sighed. "I got into a fight, okay?"

"What do you mean you got into a fight?" I exclaimed, louder than expected. Several coworkers whipped their heads towards me, now invested in my drama. Grabbing my phone, I retreated to the staff bathroom and locked the door behind me. "Shawn?" My voice echoed on tile and as I waited for Shawn's explanation, I studied a poster about organ donation hung next to the sink. Mr.

Reynolds came to mind, but I pushed that away. Not the time to ruminate about that... especially since my husband may or may not be under arrest.

"Some redneck piece of shit rear-ended me when we were stuck in traffic. Got all uppity about it. So, I punched his fucking lights out. Broke his nose too." Unmistakable pride colored the last statement.

Oh fuck. "Shawn... I understand getting pissed but, honey... you've got to control your emotions." Headlines prepopulated my mind. **FORMER NBA STAR GETS INTO ROADSIDE FISTFIGHT.** *Shawn Gilbert: Will he try boxing next?*

"Rachel," he said, his voice icy and curt, "No offense but you don't know what the fuck you're talking about."

"Babe, that's not what I—"

He cut me off. "Just, come get me. They towed the car. Minor damage but it still needs to go to the shop."

"Okay but—"

Click.

My mouth fell open. Shawn just hung up on me; a first. We barely argued and our rare fights were tame by any standards. Hurt feelings followed by a quick apology. We never yelled. No raised voices. He'd never hung up on me.

Except...

He just did.

My vision blurred—from tears or lightheadedness, I wasn't sure. My chest hitched, clenching painfully near my sternum. Shawn's face swirled in my mind and rather than bringing me comfort; it stirred up concerns. Little things, especially when taken separately. Grouchiness that extended far beyond his morning coffee, snappy comments, and curt answers. Bad mornings; bad days—everyone had them. Lord knew I did. He didn't smile as much as he used to and sometimes when he looked at me—usually with thinly veiled irritation—his eyes were hard and cold.

And last night...

No. Not the time to revisit that, no need to rehash his harsh words and thinly veiled insults. Sorrow gave way to bone-aching fatigue. Invisible weights tied themselves to each shoulder and I felt gravity's insidious pull. I chanced a look in the mirror. My cheekbones looked oddly sharp—a telltale clue I'd lost weight, not that I'd hopped on the scale. My scrubs hung off me, forcing me to cinch them extra tight. Puffed red skin lined my eyes—conjunctiva-tinged pink with frantic threads.

Gripping the sink's edges, I leaned forward and stared into the depths of my reflection. I looked like shit warmed over but... like I'd done a hundred times in my career after the horrible cases, I clenched my jaw and forced my breathing to slow. At first, my heart raced, beating clear into my ears—its sound further compounding my anxiety spiral. I persisted. Slow inhale in. I pictured the muscles between my ribs flaring outwards as my lungs filled with rich, clean air. Held it. One. Two. Three. Four. Exhaled, slow but purposeful and I imagined red globs of stress riding the molecules of carbon dioxide out. Again. Again. And like a car lurching into a lower gear—it *clicked*, and I regained control of my emotions.

Turning the tap on, I splashed ice-cold water on my face with far less finesse than an actor in a Noxzema commercial. The abrupt temperature change grounded me, bringing me back to reality. Thankfully years of witnessing devastation and death had forced me to cultivate such techniques. When the doctor called the time of death on a peds patient, we all wanted to crumble to pieces but—there were more patients to take care of. You learned to stop the emotions from creeping in, stopping them from overwhelming you—someone could die if you made a simple mistake because you were sad. Early on, I learned to stuff such feelings down and *just breathe.*

I fixed my face with a smile that felt plastic but looked authentic enough in the mirror. Unlocking the door, I sought out the charge nurse, finding her shoulder deep in the muttering, "Motherfucker."

I cleared my throat and willed my expression to be concerned but not overly so. "Meghan, Shawn just called me. His—uh—car broke down and he needs a ride. Sorry to bail on the department but I gotta go."

She turned, flicking her eyes to my face, then down where she continued rummaging in the hospital delivery system's bowels. "It's fine. Family is more important than this shithole anyway. Go pick him up. And you know what? Take the rest of your shift off too. Have some wine and drink five glasses for me, 'kay? I'll live vicariously through you."

My face twisted with what I hoped passed as gratitude. "Thanks! I'll do that *just* for you. Um... do you need help before I go?" I asked, pointing.

Meghan waved her available arm. "Nah. It's fine. Pharmacy sent Room 11's lifesaving medication down and now it's stuck in the fucking tube system while the poor guy swirls the drain. Just a normal Wednesday. Get going while the going's good!"

I quickly rattled off report, giving her the info on my patients. "Thanks again!" I called back, already halfway out the ambulance bay double doors. Fingers of poison squeezed my chest again when I climbed into my car and fired up the engine, about to shift into drive. Then I realized; I had no idea where the Denver Police Department was. I never thought I'd need to know but—my husband was there, maybe in custody... especially if his bad attitude continued. Tapping my phone's screen, I searched the address and directions. Grabbing the gearshift, I paused and a chill shot through me, despite the sun's afternoon assault—made more potent thanks to the elevation.

My throat clicked.

Who was my husband becoming?

And why?

26

Dr. Absinthe

C LAIRE TOSSED SOMETHING ON my desk. "This fax came for
you."

Turning away from my computer, I picked up the packet
of papers still warm from the fax machine. "Thanks." The
cover page read: Aubrey Landis autopsy results. My heart
thudded against my ribs, and I shakily turned the page. A
diagram of a naked woman in the anatomical position greeted
me, her head absolutely riddled with scribbles. I examined
the accompanying text: *Temporal bone skull fracture; epidural
hematoma; several small subarachnoid hemorrhages and—*

My throat clicked.

A cerebellar hemorrhage.

Scrolling further down, the autopsy listed a few other
things: which teeth had dental fillings, some surgical pins
noted in the left ankle—souvenir from a skiing accident in her
youth, and a completely unremarkable, intact chip implanted
at the base of the skull. Cause of death: cerebral edema
secondary to multiple intracranial hemorrhages, caused by
self-inflicted blunt force trauma.

Had I caused this? When I turned her inhibition settings down, had I inadvertently made things worse? I glanced down at the time of death: 6:31 p.m. Only hours after I'd made the changes.

"Shit," I muttered. My phone buzzed and I picked it up. "Yeah?" I asked distractedly, unable to take my eyes off the autopsy report.

"Shawn Gilbert's here for his appointment," Billie said.

I grabbed the autopsy report and shoved it in my desk drawer where I kept my delicate files hidden away. For my eyes only. "Thanks. Send him in."

After exchanging pleasantries, we lapsed into silence broken only by the jittering of his leg and the twirling pen in my hand—a self-soothing habit I'd picked up in med school. I was sorely in need of soothing today. Shawn sat sullenly in the cushioned chair, keeping his eyes trained on his hands. He reminded me of a kid sitting outside the principal's office; maintaining silence so as not to incriminate himself.

Rachel called me on her way to the police station and immediately after we hung up, I called Morgan, my ex, who—in the great tradition of sapphic exes—was still a good friend of mine. And more importantly, a lawyer. It helped that the man Shawn assaulted had two illegal guns on his person as well as assault rifles in the back of his truck—along with materials that could be used to make homemade bombs and a sprawling document reeking of psychotic manifesto. All in all, the fall out could have been far worse, and the cops essentially let Shawn go with a slap on the wrist. But Shawn's behavior worried me. And based on the tightness of Rachel's voice; she was concerned too.

The wall clock ticked loudly, kept company by college degrees, my medical diploma, and Board Certifications hanging in my office. Otherwise, my office was sparsely decorated. A fancy wooden desk of unknown origin had been my one splurge. Three frames adorned its top. My mother—before her body gnarled with inactivity as her nerves committed systematic and brutal suicide—smiling up at the camera, extending a glass of red wine towards the lens like she wanted to cheer her good fortune... how quickly that fucking changed. A photo of Spooky as a kitten—his black fur voluminous and ratty as if he'd stuck a claw in an electrical socket.

And a new one:

Taylor, her arm slung across my shoulders, fingers curled in a coolly casual way, brushing against the tops of my breasts—something that drove me wild. We'd grown closer, especially after I confided in her about my concerns with the chips, keeping her apprised of the happenings. We exchanged regular and nauseating I-love-yous. Most lesbians U-Hauled after the second date and so far, we'd refrained—although more and more I was entertaining the idea—so adding her photo to my office felt appropriate. My lips curled as I took her in. Absolutely gorgeous.

"Aldea?"

I pulled my attention away from the photo. "Huh?"

Shawn wearily swiped at his eyes. "What did you want to talk about?"

What the hell did he think I wanted to talk about—his opinion on the Denver Nuggets' chances this season? "I wanted to talk about what happened yesterday, Shawn."

"What do you mean?" he asked.

Playing dumb? Seriously? A kernel of anger bloomed. "What do I mean?" I leaned forward. "Maybe we could talk about how you punched a guy's lights out yesterday? Remember that little incident? Ringing any bells?"

"He rear-ended me." His bottom lip pooched out and irrational rage spiked within me.

"Christ. People get rear-ended all the time. It was a fucking accident," I said.

His chocolate eyes widened. "I wonder if it was an accident." He scoffed, an ugly sound.

"You think he did it on purpose?" I asked.

"I don't know. Maybe. He seemed self-righteous about the whole thing." He massaged his temples with his index and middle fingers. "And I don't know... I just went nutso—I lost control, but I wasn't upset about it. It was like... the fury felt—" Shawn halted, a stricken expression pinching his face.

My mouth went bone dry. "What?" I asked.

His forehead wrinkled. "It felt fucking amazing. Justified." Shawn wrung his hands. "I dunno. It's hard to explain. I remember him being a fuck and getting pissed off. I remember how his face crumpled under my fist then—" Fingers grazed his thick beard, and he stared at the ceiling intently, as if searching for something. "I don't really remember much after that."

"What do you mean?" Ice coursed through my veins. "Like it's all a blur?" I asked. That I could understand. It happened to me all the time. Driving home from the hospital singing along with 80s hits, not seeing the passing scenery but taking the correct turns home without conscious thought.

He shook his head. "No. It's a black hole. The next thing I remember was the blue and red lights—someone called 911."

Even if he didn't recall, Morgan told me Shawn beat the man to a bloody pulp; definitely more than a simple punch to the nose. Broken mandible—bad enough for a maxillofacial surgeon to wire it shut for six weeks. Fractured teeth embedded in the gumline, and a collapsed lung thanks to a rib snapping like a twig—its sharp end puncturing spongy tissue, letting air loose in the thoracic cavity.

Untreated, it would have collapsed completely, could even cause a cardiac arrest. Luckily, some adrenaline junkie ER doc ramrodded a tube through his chest wall and re-inflated the lung. Such injuries suggested a real ass-kicking; verified by cellphone footage of the altercation Morgan got ahold of, greasing the appropriate palms to keep press out of the loop. Not for the first time I thanked my lucky stars our split was amicable.

"You don't remember... anything?" I asked.

"Nothing."

I studied him while he contemplated his hands. I didn't think he was lying. Shawn never struck me as a liar, and I'd gotten pretty good at sniffing them out during my years of practice. Patients feigning illness to score disability benefits. People trying to game the system, like Dora Sale trying to score benzos. "How do you feel now?" I asked.

"Tired. So fucking tired of this shit. Like... I can't do anything right. I finally—" he slammed his fists on the desk, and I jumped "—*finally* get things going my way. New chip, new me, but it's not enough. I'm too rash, too reactionary. Listen, I'm just doing what any guy would do. You think other people would shake the guy's hand, 'aw shucks, no harm, no foul'? Fuck no. But I get persecuted for it. *Shawn should be perfect*; it's like I'm back in school again, getting my ass ripped for getting a B or missing a free throw. Like... can't you and Rachel cut me a fucking break?" His shoulders drooped and he deflated, like someone—me and Rachel apparently—let the air out of him.

I felt for him, I really did. But I still... I wondered if his reactions were situational or an issue with the chip. "Listen, I'm going to postpone our trip, at least a week so you can get some rest, huh? No use in burning the candle at both ends," I said.

"No, I'm not wimping out on you. We're going," he replied.

I acquiesced despite my better judgement.

27

Rachel

WITH A FEW MINUTES left on my lunch break—my husband on my mind—I stole away from the ER, carefully avoiding any coworker who might ask "for a hand" which would invariably turn into me helping clean off a patient covered head-to-toe in feces… before I was on the clock. Not again. Hands thrust in my scrub pants, I made my way out to the ambulance bay and remarkably, found it empty. No diesel fumes choking me while I pondered or respiratory therapists puffing away on cancer sticks. Crisp mountain air filled my nostrils and I inhaled deeply, shutting my eyes. Dr. Absinthe's stupid commercial rose unbidden—an annoying earworm I subconsciously heard a thousand times a shift playing on the ER patient room TVs. I shoved it away.

Shawn. I pulled my phone from my pocket and held it near my mouth. "Siri, call Shawn," I said.

"Calling Shawn," Siri confirmed in that coolly efficient voice of hers. I resisted the urge to chew on my thumbnail—a nervous habit of mine I'd (mostly) broken—as I waited and made myself think about the antibiotic resistant bacteria caked underneath.

"Hello?" Shawn answered. Flight announcements peppered the background.

"Hey babe, you just land?" I asked.

Snatches of conversation flowed past. "Yep. Flight wasn't too bad, but some woman kept yelling about a gremlin on the wing." He chuckled. "Of course, she was insanely drunk and probably saw that episode of *Twilight Zone* as a kid."

"Seriously?"

"Dead serious."

Having worked in the ER my entire nursing career, I couldn't say I was surprised. And instead of having access to medications—sedatives and antipsychotics among them—flight attendants had to make do with duct tape. "People are really something, aren't they?" I asked.

"You ain't kidding. Sometimes I think the shit you tell me about work is crazy and then I see somethin' like that in the wild."

I traced the craggy, snow-capped mountain in the distance, the outline of a shaggy buffalo.

"What's your plan for the rest of the day?" I asked. Tomorrow was their interview but there was still plenty of daylight, especially in Los Angeles.

"Sorry, 'scuse me," Shawn said to an unseen passerby—voice slightly muffled—before turning his attention back to me. "Taking a car to the hotel." He dropped his voice. "The Beverly Hilton Hotel; where Whitney died... which I found kind of morbid but whatever." Something aggressively beeping—a luggage cart or shuttle—raced past him. "Then we're going to Nobu. I think Aldea wants to see a Kardashian in the wild and the producers snagged us reservations."

"Just don't leave me for Khloe if you see her. She has a thing for ball players."

He laughed. "Don't worry. I'm more of a Kim K kind of dude."

"I know. Hey—" I hesitated "—uh, how is Aldea doing?"

"Fine. She's been texting Taylor all day. Sounds like it's getting kind of serious," Shawn remarked. "On the flight—when the lady wasn't losing her shit—she was asking me how long it took us to move in together. She's thinking about it."

Finding out about Taylor was a welcome surprise. I wasn't blind; Aldea Absinthe was hot. I noticed. Shawn noticed. Nearly every employee of the ER noticed. Her mere presence produced massive gay panic amongst the sapphic leaning ladies. Realizing the hot smart doctor traveling with my husband had no interest in him in *that* way was nice. "That's awesome! They're great together," I remarked. And they were. We'd gone out for drinks with them at a local brewery recently and it was obvious they were in love. Long lingering looks, footsie under the table, and holding hands.

An ambulance swerved into the bay—lights and sirens. It never failed.

"Lucky you. I gotta go, a rig just pulled up. Be safe and have fun, okay? I love you!"

"Love you back, babe," Shawn replied, acting like his old self again.

Medics swarmed from the ambulance like efficient ants—a Lucas device performing CPR while a medic held an Ambu bag, giving it a squeeze every six seconds. Phone went in pocket, and I pulled my hair up in a tight bun. Time to get back to work while my hubby was galivanting about LA.

28

Dr. Absinthe

I TOOK A SWIG of beer and the fermented barley joined up with the decadent sushi I'd savored for dinner—spicy tuna nigiri and yellowtail sashimi. Simple but delicious. No celebrities were seated at the tables around us—at least, no one I recognized. The meal left me comfortably full and a bit sleepy but instead of falling into the cozy hotel bed as planned, I found myself at AVALON Hollywood. In the VIP section. In my very own booth. Well... Shawn's and Baylon's booth. Your standard neurologist didn't have a hope in hell of scoring their own VIP booth. Maybe if I were a world-renowned plastic surgeon skilled in rhinoplasties and boob jobs of the rich and famous, I could snag my own booth.

"Having fun?" Shawn asked, raising his voice to be heard over the thudding beat.

I considered the question. During my med school days—when I was young and full of energy—I'd thought I died and went to heaven, being at a famous Hollywood club watching one of my favorite DJs at the turntables. And I sure as hell wouldn't have been caught dead sitting. Old Aldea would be on the dance floor, swaying in time with the rhythm pouring from the speakers. New Aldea? A nice shower then throwing on comfy PJs, followed by cuddles under the covers watching TV sounded more my speed.

Too bad Taylor was states away... not that we would do much cuddling, not right off the bat anyway. "Yeah, it's fun," I answered, taking another sip of beer. "Where's Baylon?"

Shawn rolled his eyes. "Off trying to get laid if I had to guess. He hasn't changed one bit—not that I would want him to." Shawn leaned in and gave me a conspiratorial smile. "Once, when we were on the road, he picked up this girl that gave him crabs. We made him boxer shorts that said *Baylon's Crab Shack*. He didn't find it very funny."

Another bonus of a committed loving relationship; the incidence of crabs went down exponentially. "That's funny," I replied, involuntarily imagining Baylon naked and scratching his crotch with gusto.

"Yep," Shawn said, untangling his long frame from the booth. He stood, earning appreciative glances from the table next to ours—a bachelorette party if the Bride to Be sash was to be trusted. "Speaking of Baylon and his crabs, I'm gonna go see if I can find him. You need anything?"

I held my beer bottle up, still half full. "Nah, I'm good, thanks."

"Be right back," Shawn said, and he took off, weaving through throngs of partygoers.

Tiësto scaled the BPM back and the unmistakable notes of *Silence* swelled, joined by Sarah McLachlan's ethereal voice. As it always did, as if I were nothing more than Pavlov's dog, my heart clenched painfully, and just like that—I was back in my mother's ICU room, holding her clawed hand while trance music piped in from my headphones, soothing my soul.

Despite the high dose IV steroids, IVIG, and plasmapheresis—Mom continued to worsen. And thanks to rampant nosocomial infections, she landed in the ICU. Unable to manage her own secretions—a trial of thickened liquids resulted in a nasty bout of aspiration pneumonia and the doctors deemed her NPO indefinitely—a surgeon inserted a feeding tube. Her only sustenance came from clay colored liquid pumped into the G-tube.

Before my very eyes, she became a skeletal shell. A shadow. Despite the nurses' best efforts, tender skin over bony pressure points flowered into decubitus ulcers that wept fluid and became a breeding ground for bacteria. And like a baby she messed herself, having lost voluntary control of her bowels and bladder. To ease the breakdown of skin from urine and fecal matter, they'd inserted a urinary catheter and a rectal tube. Except... then she battled UTI after UTI, and the antibiotics needed to combat the germs escalated as they grew more resistant and lethal.

The most disheartening part of it all? Most people went to the ICU to *get better* but my mom—with her diagnosis of ALS—would *never* get better. No. Her disease was a death sentence. Death by lethal injection, electric chair, firing squad, or even a guillotine, was kinder than her fate. At least *those* folks had the comfort of a last meal: steak with lobster or maybe fried chicken with a heaping helping of buttery mashed potatoes. Such delicacies would only choke her, hastening her demise.

Her disease progressed at an alarming rate. Breathing became a chore; something once so easy and mindless. Diaphragm weakened, and her team of doctors said that if she worsened, she'd require a breathing tube and since there was minimal hope she'd ever get better, we were looking at a tracheostomy. I knew it wasn't something she wanted: a massive hole cut in her neck, just like those anti-smoking commercials where a decrepit woman inhaled blue curling cigarette smoke through her stoma, speaking in a robotic voice—all gravel and phlegm. My mother couldn't live without a ventilator pumping in oxygen, removing poisonous carbon dioxide. Forever reliant on machines. Waiting for Death to show mercy and claim her. And in my experience; Death was far too slow for those suffering.

After the doctors bestowed their grim news and departed to another ailing patient's bedside, my mother marshalled her strength and motioned with a curled finger—Herculean effort put into the minor movement. I leaned in and put my ear to her mouth. Even up close, I strained to hear the words she struggled mightily to say—the stale puffs of air from her mouth meager at best. "*Kill... me. Kill... me. Please.*" The last words my mother ever spoke aloud. A request. A wish. A demand.

At first, I recoiled, disgusted by the thought of taking a life—her life, my mother's life—even if *that* was what she so desired. Exhausted by the effort of speaking, she lapsed into blessed unconsciousness.

With my music and the steady beeping of her monitors keeping me company, I mulled it over, examining it like a grueling math problem from my one of my undergrad classes. She didn't deserve to suffer—that much was clear—and my mother's dignity was rapidly bleeding away as her body betrayed her. And she would never get better. The stark truth was this was as good as my mother would get. It was all downhill from here. *First, do no harm*, echoed in my skull, doubling and reverberating. Words we'd repeated during my white coat ceremony at the beginning of medical school.

First, do no harm. While my mother was still technically alive, she lived Hell on Earth. Each day filled with suffering, pain, despair. Hopelessness. *That was harm enough.* By the end of the day, I made my decision. Mercy. Mercy was the answer.

The overhead lights were off and—other than chimes and alarms from monitors and IV pumps rooms away—it was quiet. Scattered yellow checkers shone in from outside; people on night shift or insomniacs struggling in vain to find Mr. Sandman. Dawn was hours away and I could just make out twinkling stars high in the sky—those not completely washed out by city lights.

The heavens above were indifferent to humanity's suffering, to my mother's never-ending pain, and I failed to recognize their beauty. Instead of feeling wonder, I internally raged over the injustice of it all. I thought of my ER rotations, seeing people use and abuse their bodies with drugs, alcohol, and cigarettes. The ER staff had a saying: *you can't kill a cockroach.* And it was true. Someone who had no true value to society could get into a car accident at 95 miles per hour and walk away unscathed but a person who paid their taxes and worked tirelessly might step in the crosswalk and get mowed down by one of the useless; dead on arrival.

Tearing my eyes from the sky, I looked around her room one last time, taking everything in and fixing it in my mind though the very act pained me. An aseptic scent of bandages and gauze hung in the air, joined by the sickly-sweet rot of sickness carried with each of my mother's paltry exhalations. Dying from the inside out. Rotting. Her paper chart hung from the foot of the bed with bright red lettering proclaiming **DNR**. No CPR. No lifesaving measures. No breaking ribs in a futile effort to prolong a poor-quality life. She'd suffered enough.

Tears brimmed in my eyes and my chest ached, cored out and hollowed—as if someone scooped out my heart, leaving a cold abyss in its wake—and I bent down. Pressing my lips to her clammy forehead, I took care to brush thin hair from her brow. Returning the nighttime kisses from my childhood but with the roles reversed. Now, I was the one caring for my mother, offering love and comfort.

Instead of her perfume, I smelled death and stale urine. "I love you," I whispered.

Her eyes fluttered but she didn't wake.

Before I lost my nerve, I pressed the pillow to her face. At first the pressure was delicate, almost hesitant, but then I drew on a reservoir of strength deep within. I pushed harder, choking off what little oxygen she managed to inhale. Tears streamed down my cheeks, falling to the sheets, leaving small wet dots.

It was over quickly. She didn't even struggle. Her chest quieted and I returned to my uncomfortable chair near the window and resumed the music while I silently cried. It was all I had left. Once the song ended, I hit the call light and when they answered, I told them she was gone.

"Hey Aldea!"

I yanked myself out of the cruel memory and looked up. Shawn grinned down at me. His eyes were bright and too wide. Strobe lights flashed, giving me a glimpse of white just underneath his nose. As if feeling my eyes on him, he brushed underneath his nostrils, giving a gusty sniff. Whatever was there—cocaine if I had to guess—disappeared. Baylon stood next to Shawn, sweat beading from his forehead and he fidgeted. "Everything okay, Shawn?" I asked. I tipped my beer into my mouth and swallowed the liquid. My trip down memory lane went on longer than I thought—my beer had gone warm.

Shawn bared blindingly white teeth at me. "Never better! Baylon introduced me to some very nice people." Nice people with drugs apparently. While part of me wanted to scream at him: *how dare you get blitzed and compromise my chips?*—I knew I couldn't. I was his doctor, sure, but somewhere along the way, the lines blurred. We'd gone on double dates. Drank together. I mean, here I was in a club with him, pissed off he was having a good time for once.

Still... we should go. "Say, you want to get out of—" I started.

"Hey babe, let me buy you a drink?" cut me off. "Then maybe a dance and... who knows?"

I sought out the voice's owner and found him in the VIP booth next to ours. He waggled bushy eyebrows at me and favored me with a lecherous grin that made my skin crawl.

"No thank you," I responded politely, turning away.

A rough hand grasped my arm, pulling it back with more force than necessary. "Listen, don't be a bitch. I'm just trying to be nice." His voice had a hint of purr, but the words were harsh and dripping with poison.

"I said, *no*," I said as I stood, struggling to wrench my arm from his grasp. Like a leech, he held on.

Shawn hissed, "Let her go, asshole."

"Make me," the guy said, instantly transporting me back to kindergarten where schoolyard taunts ruled. *Make me*? Then... regressing completely back to grade school, he poked his tongue out at Shawn and waggled it. "Do it you pussy—"

Wrong move.

Shawn's fist made its acquaintance with the dude's face and even over the music, I heard a painful *crunch* as his nose crumpled inwards. All the tone went out of his body, and he slumped to the floor. Totally out of commission. *Shawn must have a thing for breaking noses*, I thought ruefully through my panic.

"Fucking prick," Shawn muttered. His eyes were narrowed to slits, reminding me of a coiled cobra intent on a fatal strike.

Baylon looked how I felt: mouth agape, eyes wide and disbelieving. "Bro... this ain't good," he moaned, putting his hands to his temples.

"We gotta go," I said, eyes darting about. The creep had been sitting table alone, no doubt trying to lure young drunk women into his clutches, and no one seemed to notice the altercation, all too caught up in the music or their own conquests. The bachelorette party had abandoned their booth in favor of the dancefloor long ago and I thanked our lucky stars for it.

Shawn growled, "I ought to kick the living shit out of him," and picked up his right foot, planting his Timberland in the man's ribs as if marking his target. The man groaned. Shawn cocked his leg back and given the dark look on his face, he planned on doing just that: kicking the living shit out of the dude.

"No, no, no. We gotta go. NOW," I admonished, grabbing Shawn's arm. His eyes flashed and for a second, I worried he'd turn his wrath on me. But as quickly as the fire rose, it dimmed and he nodded, following me.

I heard him mutter under his breath, "Should've killed that fucking prick," and I tried to reassure myself he'd just gotten protective of me and with alcohol and cocaine in his system, overreacted. But even then, I knew I was lying to myself.

29

Rachel

NORMALLY, 7 P.M. MARKED when I *left* the hospital—assuming I got out on time—but I was home, lounging in cozy sweatpants and padding around in tie-dye Crocs Shawn always teased me about. My hubby was off hanging out with Lewis, watching NCAA basketball, and eating fried food. As for me? It was day two off work, and I was enjoying every second of it. I'd already putzed around the apartment and watered brown-spotted plants brought from Texas neglected for far too long, watched mindless TV, and caught up on my reading. Nothing medical. Instead, I was deeply immersed in a spicy passage where the hunky knight—packed full of muscle, positively oozing testosterone—ripped his fair maiden's dress off, so incensed by her beauty. Problematic? Sure. Smutty as hell? Absolutely. Right at the juicy part, where a throbbing member came into play, my phone rang. Jess' name flashed across the screen. I considered letting it go to voicemail; most of the time someone calling from work wanted a favor, usually in the form of shift coverage.

But guilt got the better of me. "Hello?" I said, eyes still skimming the pages of my book. The lady was about to get herself a hot beef injection. The knight still had his armor on—except for the cod piece, of course.

"Oh my God, Rachel, I'm so sorry for calling and bothering you. I know you're on a string of days off, but I didn't know who else to call! Everyone else is either already working or told me to pretty much fuck off," Jess exclaimed, the words tumbling out in a breathless rush. Her voice brimmed with tears. She tended towards the dramatic at the best of times but to be fair, always got horrible patients who enjoyed tossing literal shit at her head.

I closed the book and let out a sigh; I wasn't finishing it tonight. "Jess, it's fine. What's up?"

As if giving Jess permission—she unleashed a floodgate of tears. She spoke haltingly, taking in gulps of air between sobs, "It's Louie. He spiked a temp at daycare today. Which... whatever, he's a kid. They're always fucking sick. Germ factories. But just 20 minutes ago, he came and told me he had an... an... accident." She let out another hitching sob, winding up to a wail. "Sorry. It's just... so fucking bad! Accident isn't even the word for what happened. I walked into his room and there was puke and shit *everywhere*. And when I say everywhere, I mean EVERYWHERE. Shit smeared on the walls, puddles of puke on the floor and in his bed. I don't even know where to begin." She let out a rueful laugh devoid of humor. "Honestly, I should probably burn the house down. Listen, I hate to ask you but..."

I cut in, "I'll cover your shift. Don't even worry about it. You caught me before my first glass of wine. I'll probably have less puke and shit to deal with at work than you do at home." Mentally, I applauded my decision not to have children... at least at work I got paid to clean up excrement. Unfolding my legs, I got up from my comfy easy chair and walked to the bedroom. I wasn't exactly wild about night shifts, having put in my time as a rookie nurse. All the crazies appeared en masse during the late hours and if was a full moon? Forget it—the place was an absolute shitshow and everyone acted like a cat in a bathtub.

"You're a lifesaver. Thank you, thank you, thank you! Seriously I'll repay the favor. Starbucks gift card? Massage? Need someone to disappear, not questions asked? Anything! You name it."

I flapped my hand, not that Jess could see. "Don't worry about it. I know how it goes. I'll keep you in mind the next time I have a bug and need some coverage, okay? Now go clean up that disaster in your house. And... good luck."

Jess snickered. "Thanks again. I need the luck, trust me."

Luckily for *me*, the moon hanging overhead was a mere sliver, nothing like the dreaded full moon. Still... I gazed at it mistrustfully as I walked across the parking lot, as if it might engorge and become full before my very eyes. The last thing I needed was psychotic meth-heads howling at the damn thing. Early in my career medics brought in an elderly man with dementia, and he sat up on the cot baying like a bloodhound as a jaundiced, engorged moon hung in the sky behind him. I was certain I was about to be eaten by a lycanthrope, but we soon realized he was septic as hell from a UTI and delirious with fever. Every time I saw a full moon, I couldn't help but remember that encounter.

Even with no full moon, the ER was a disaster. A patient in each treatment room, a packed waiting room, and patients languishing in hallway beds and—failing that—chairs if they were well enough. After clocking in, I jumped headlong into the foray, walking from room to room—starting IVs, drawing labs, passing meds. When I got a moment to breathe and check my watch, it was well past 1 a.m. and by some miracle; we'd nearly cleared the board. Only three patients left in the entire ER.

"Rachel! You want to take lunch now?" called out the night charge, Becky. She held a mug filled—presumably—with coffee. On the front: a cartoon man bound and gagged with Christmas lights, the words *Silent Night* above him. Scattered off to the side of the man were empty vials of Propofol and Ativan.

One of the rare perks of night shift: time for a proper lunch. "I won't say no to lunch!" I called back cheerfully.

"Thirty minutes!" Becky playfully tapped her watch. "Tick-tock."

"Hey, that's better than the no minutes of lunch I'm used to!" I retorted.

I found the breakroom blissfully empty. A small TV played in the corner, turned to a station that—at this time of night—churned out infomercials. An obnoxiously bubbly woman touted some miracle product guaranteed to change your life! Walking to the fridge, I extracted my lunch box. Today's fare: a Granny Smith apple, Twizzlers, and old faithful—a protein bar. With a grunt, I flopped down on one of the flimsy plastic chairs. I bit into my apple and chewed, pulling out my phone and clicking on the Facebook app.

It didn't load. Piece of shit work Wi-Fi.

Setting my phone down next to the Twizzlers, I thought of Shawn. The show went without a hitch, both him and Aldea playing their appropriate parts, talking up the chip. Aldea seemed more relaxed this go-round and Shawn... well, Shawn was Shawn. I'd watched the episode with him when he got back but instead of being excited, he seemed oddly withdrawn. He kept his eyes glued to the screen but didn't pay it any attention. Instead, his expression was glazed, and he absentmindedly stroked his right hand, hissing when he applied too much pressure. I didn't notice any bruises—but I thought the knuckles a bit swollen.

"What happened?" I'd asked, gently grasping his hand, and examining it. Small abrasions crisscrossed the knuckles and like I'd forced him to touch a hot stove burner, he yanked it away with a wounded look on his face.

He trained his eyes down and mumbled, "Nothing."

Nothing. Bullshit. I'd fired off a quick text to Aldea, asking her how the trip went.

Fine. That was it. *Fine.*

Unbidden, Mr. Reynolds rose in my mind. My stomach twisted and I stared at my half-eaten apple, already browning in the breakroom's canned air. Appetite gone. And wasn't that how it went? I finally had time to eat and couldn't bring myself to do so. I left the rest of my food untouched and clocked back in. Might as well get paid for being here.

"Hey Rachel, you busy?" someone yelled from the major resuscitation room. A screech followed the question like punctuation. By the sounds of it, it was either a sick patient, someone on drugs, a mix of the two, or someone smashed a hamster with a cast iron skillet.

I popped my head through the curtain and took in the scene. A diaphoretic man covered in oozing sores writhed on the cot and two massive, muscle-bound medics held him in place while Kim started an IV. "What do you need?" I asked, thankful—for once—I hadn't drawn the short straw of patient assignments.

"For starters, a Costco application for myself. But some restraints would be nice!" Kim replied as she secured his IV with medical tape and blue Coban.

I laughed. "Restraints and Costco application, coming right up!" Off I went to the ER's supply room, where I snatched up the last package of restraints, delivering them into Kim's grateful hands. "Need anything else?

"Nah, we got it," Kim answered.

The patient let out another scream; all scalded baby plunged into a far-too-hot bath. The scream cut off and the patient peppered the outburst with "CUNT!" earning synchronized eyerolls from Kim and myself.

I gave her a quick thumbs up, then strolled by the charge nurse desk. "We're out of restraints in the supply room," I said.

Becky rolled her eyes and sighed. "Naturally. Everyone is high on meth these days, so we've been blowing through 'em like hot cakes." She reached into one of her many scrub pockets and extracted a ring of keys. "Do you mind running to the central supply room and grabbing more?"

Another explosion of noise sounded from the resuscitation room. Something plastic hit the wall, followed by a meaty *thud* and liquid splashing on the floor. "DO NOT THROW THE URINAL!" Then... "My God, look at this fucking mess."

"I really dodged a bullet with that one," I murmured, grabbing the keys.

"Yeah, you did. But Kim can handle that douche," Becky replied. "Use the key with the red around it; gets you into any room in the hospital."

I nodded, grabbing the keys with a jangle and off I went.

At night, the halls were deserted—a stark contrast to daytime when noise filled the corridors, reminding me of the local zoo's aviary where colorful birds chirped and flapped about. But now? Total ghost town. Each of my steps were oddly loud and echoed off the walls, doubling, and tripling in intensity. Briefly, I fought off an urge to yell, "Hello!" like a tourist standing above the Grand Canyon.

I thought back to my clinicals in nursing school and how staff whispered about a nun stalking the halls after midnight. My preceptor swore up and down she'd seen the habit-clad woman lingering by the elevator, peering about with coal-black eyes. At the time, I'd laughed off the ghost stories, chalking it up to bored old-timers messing with fresh meat. In the wee hours of morning though, during the witching hour... I found it easier to buy into. I walked faster, fighting the urge to break into a run. The keys jingled in my sweat slicked palm.

"Rachel, stop being such a puss. It's *fine*," I whispered to myself, keeping my eyes focused directly ahead, fearful if I looked elsewhere, I'd see a pale, rotting face staring at me from beneath a tattered habit.

Why on God's green Earth was central supply so damn far from the ER? After an eternity of walking with prickling fear nipping at my heels, I finally reached my destination. And true to Becky's word, the red key turned easily, allowing me access to the massive room. It took minutes of searching through the medical supplies haphazardly strewn about before locating the restraints, hidden under some bed pans. I grabbed an armful and pulled the door shut behind me.

Rather than returning the way I came, I swung left, taking a detour that shaved a few minutes from the trip. Mounted to the wall on my right was a red arrow that pointed the way to several outpatient offices: Dermatology, Surgery, and—

I paused.

And... to Neurology. To Dr. Absinthe's office. In the middle of the night. With not a soul around.

Internally I warred with myself. It would be *so easy* to take a quick peek. But... was it the right thing to do? Eh... *it wasn't exactly wrong*, I reasoned. What would I be hurting? I considered, building up my courage. I wasn't a prude by any means and wasn't infatuated with following rules and regulations. In high school, I'd done my fair share of sneaking out to parties, nearly dying of alcohol poisoning every other weekend. Once, I'd swiped a lipstick from the drugstore, but the guilt nearly crippled me. Kleptomania wasn't for me.

Should I use the master key? Let myself into Dr. Absinthe's office? Just to look around—it wasn't like I was going to *steal* anything. Well... except for maybe information—assuming I found any.

I thought of Shawn's withdrawn behavior and not-so-subtle personality changes. Mr. Reynolds with his seizures, nasty brain bleed, and subsequent death.

They had that damned migraine chip in common and that decided me.

I slid the key into the lock. Palms sweating, I turned it, fearful it might stick. I held my breath. It rotated easily. "Phew," I muttered, exhaling with relief.

As expected, the office was shrouded in darkness. The reception desk was vacant and the TV that normally played Dr. Absinthe's commercial over and over was black and silent. What if someone had been in the office? Should I pretend to be housekeeping? Say, *looks like I took the wrong turn to*

Albuquerque? like Bugs Bunny making a quip while munching on a carrot?

I deposited the restraints on the closest waiting room chair, hoping no one would notice my prolonged absence from the ED. I could always say I had a nasty bout of diarrhea if someone asked, I supposed. No one questioned a case of the Hershey Squirts. Squinting through the murk, I made my way to the door adjacent to the receptionist's desk that led to the back where the exam rooms and procedure room were.

And Dr. Absinthe's office.

Feeling like an inexperienced cat burglar, I quietly opened doors and peeked inside each.

Exam room. Exam room. A closet filled with boxes of free samples and supplies.

Then... pay dirt: Dr. Absinthe's office.

Tiptoeing inside, I shut the door behind me softly, jumping when the latch reengaged. "Get ahold of yourself, Rachel," I whispered. I scanned the books, unsure of what I was looking for. Part of me hoped I'd come across a book titled: *My Migraine Chips and My Nefarious Plans* but each book appeared consistent with standard medical texts doctors displayed in their offices like a mighty hunter did with taxidermized heads of their kills. Tomes filled with neurologic disorders and clinical, sterile language that would put the worst insomniac to sleep, neuro-anatomy atlases, and on the top shelf—diplomas, and degrees that proclaimed: *Yes, I have a medical degree. See? Trust me, I'm a doctor.*

Turning from the bookshelf, I focused my attention on the desk. It was gorgeous, made of a quality wood; mahogany if I had to guess but I didn't know shit about wood. In gold, a nameplate proclaimed: *Dr. Aldea Absinthe MD*, and next to that was a picture frame of Dr. Absinthe with her arms slung around a frail woman's shoulders. Her mother if I had to guess. A photo of Taylor. Another of Spooky. A few awards sat off to the side, not front in center because that would be too ostentatious. Leaning close, I made out *Resident of the Year* in silver lettering.

Otherwise, the desktop was sparse.

Crouching—knees crackling with the effort—I opened desk drawers. Office supplies. Stacks of papers with repeating 0s and 1s—code? The smallest drawer contained protein bars and a dusty Snickers still in its package.

Sighing with disappointment, I slid the drawer shut but it stuck and caught on something. Frowning, I opened the drawer again and found something sticking up that hadn't been there a second ago.

A false back?

Carefully, I gripped the false back, pulling it up and away and a handheld notebook flopped into view. Its cover was red and unlabeled. I flipped through the pages, trepidation growing with each page. A list of patient names—everyone who'd received a chip. I glanced through the names—most I didn't recognize but a few I did.

There was Mr. Reynolds who'd gone comfort care and passed away. *Deceased.*

Matthew Willis—the name sparking recognition within me. He hadn't come in on my shift but thanks to his bizarre behavior, all the ER staff heard about him through idle gossip. They'd hauled him in, covered in blood. Drugs, they said, probably bath salts. He'd attacked his wife, ripping her throat out with his bare teeth, and had succumbed to an excited delirium despite everyone's best efforts. *Deceased.*

Two names I didn't recognize followed:

Mrs. Combs. Menopause induced migraines. *Deceased.*

Aubrey Landis. *Deceased.*

My breath caught when I saw the next page.

Shawn Gilbert. Traumatic brain injury induced migraines. And written in sharp, slanting handwriting befitting a doctor: *Fits of rage? Personality changes?*

There were more names and medical indications for the chip—greater than fifty in all. The rest of the notebook was empty, all unlined pages. With a racing mind, I replaced the notebook, but my fingers brushed against something else.

I cautiously picked it up, noting a faint tremor in my hands that sent the pages fluttering.

Autopsy reports.

I scanned them; finding each patient had died secondary to intracranial hemorrhages. And each patient... had a chip. Heart racing, I replaced the papers, ensuring the false back was firmly in place.

I retraced my steps through the entirety of the office, picking up the restraints and locked the door behind me.

It wasn't just my imagination...

Something was going on here.

30

THIRTY SECONDS AFTER RACHEL left Dr. Absinthe's office, the motion activated camera discretely placed amongst textbooks winked off.

Had she looked up, she might have seen the red light.

But she did not.

31

Dr. Absinthe

A NOTIFICATION POPPED UP on my phone, making a sharp *ding!* I snuck a look at Taylor—still passed out; exhausted from a long day of clinic—and paused *Hellraiser*. Taylor had been gung-ho about the flick—having never seen it—but lasted five minutes before sleep claimed her. Her lips curled into a faint smile and even in sleep, she was the most beautiful woman I'd ever seen. Supportive. Wonderful. My confidant, listening to my growing fears and concerns. Always offering reassurance. Love swelled within me, sending a pleasant tightening through my chest. I brushed her curly hair away from her forehead and stroked the smooth skin of her temple. She stirred, then stilled.

Wrenching my attention from Taylor, I glanced at my phone.

This late at night, the *ding* had to be the group text.

Technology was a wonderful thing, keeping me connected with friends. Despite the separation of time and countless miles—my medical school pals and I still communicated regularly. Most went into surgical specialties, and I could expect random texts from them at all hours. Even Martina—my bestie in medical school and badass ER doctor—sent me memes in the middle of the night on her night shifts. Their texts and memes alike were often disgusting, and a common theme was rectal foreign bodies;

most often stuck in middle-aged men. Anticipating a shitty joke about cucumbers or gerbils, I clicked on the notification.

My heart leapt into my throat.

Not a pithy text from a friend.

An alert from one of the motion-activated cameras I'd installed in the office, completely forgotten—until now. Months back, I'd noticed supplies going missing; innocuous stuff at first: lidocaine vials and syringes. Then free samples of medications—nothing fun like Ativan but stuff like Gabapentin or Lyrica; stuff that could still be abused. I'd contacted a security company who mounted cameras inconspicuously throughout the office and caught our office manager red-handed. I fired her and took the cameras down.

Except one.

I completely spaced on the one in my office; I'd set the camera to alert after hours and hadn't stayed late for a while. Frowning, I tapped the alert and watched the accompanying video. I'd sprung for night vision—despite the increased price—and watched the intruder with startling clarity. They had their back to the camera, obscuring their identity.

What did they want? And who thought they could waltz into *my* office in the middle of the night like they owned the place? Annoyance gave way to trepidation as I watched the intruder pull open desk drawers.

The intruder lifted my tiny red notebook from its hiding place and opened it. Thumbed through the pages. My trepidation morphed into panic.

Shit, shit, shit.

After Mr. Reynolds and Mr. Willis, I started keeping notes but didn't want them on my computer. If something were to happen, an investigation or whatever, hard drives were the first place authorities looked! Putting it down on paper—in a little throwaway notebook I kept hidden away like a teenage diary—felt appropriate. Easy to keep track of. Easy to dispose of... if needed.

My heart thudded against my ribs, tapping out an anxious rhythm that quickly gave way to anger. What the hell was going on here? My fists clenched painfully, and my cheeks grew hot.

The intruder—still faceless and nameless—put the notebook back, then pulled a sheath of papers from the drawer: the autopsy reports. Rifled through them. When they'd gotten their fill, they covered their tracks—putting everything away like they'd found it. Dark body turned towards the window and a stray moonbeam splashed over their head, enhancing features otherwise slightly muddled even with the night vision upgrade.

Pulled back hair, scrubs.

My eyes widened. Rachel?

"What?" I muttered to myself. What could she be doing? Sure, she'd questioned me with Mr. Reynolds but acquiesced easily enough. And we'd hung out since then—all four of us—and she'd seemed completely fine. All smiles and jokes; cool, calm, and relaxed.

I gingerly got off the couch, taking care to tuck the cozy gray blanket under Taylor's sleeping form. I already missed its comforting embrace. Spooky cracked open a yellow eye and let out an inquisitive *prrprrrp* as he snuggled further into Taylor's back. He'd been skeptical of her initially—still was when she came home in work scrubs reeking of other animals—but he was her little shadow now. The second she sat down; he settled in next to her, purring up a storm. Seeing them together warmed my heart. My little family.

My secrets coming to light could ruin all of that.

And I wasn't about to let that happen.

Patting Spooky's head, I murmured, "It's okay, buddy. You keep sleeping. Mommy needs to figure some stuff out." Black fur whispered underneath my fingertips, making me smile despite my anxiety. His motor revved and he drifted off, joining Taylor in dreamland.

I tiptoed to my home office, a much cozier den than my work one. The walls were adorned with pictures: some of Mom and me, others with med school friends. Framed posters hung behind the desk—all women I admired: Marie Curie, Rosalind Franklin, and my personal favorite, Roberta Bondar, an astronaut, *and* neurologist. The desk was worn, its corners chipped after countless moves. It'd been my desk as a kid, and it felt right to keep it as a reminder of where I'd started. Sentimental value, I guessed. Walking by, I stroked its surface, but the familiar woodgrain texture failed to comfort like it usually did. A steadily mounting anxiety left my arms and legs abuzz with nervous energy. A sour taste rose in my mouth, replacing the buttery popcorn I'd eaten earlier.

Rachel Gilbert knew. *She knew*. God what was I going to do? She saw the list and my jotted notes. Couple *that* with autopsy reports... how could I have been so *stupid* to write it down? And hide it in my office? Stupid. Stupid. Stupid.

I needed to talk to her, voice my concerns. She was a reasonable person, or at least, I hoped. It wasn't like I could murder her to keep my secret safe. I turned my computer on and scanned my schedule. We could meet at The Coffee Bean and chat: woman to woman. I glanced at the time: late as hell. Tomorrow, I'd text her at a more appropriate time and straighten this out.

32

Rachel

S IPPING A CHAI TEA latte while waiting for Aldea, I indulged in one of my favorite activities: people watching.

Two medical students—with matching forlorn expressions, dark circles, and a massive stack of well-thumbed through anatomy notes—frantically quizzed each other in the corner. Prepping for an exam and I sympathized with their pain. Medical school was a different brand of awful from nursing school; neither especially pleasant. Nursing and medical students keep the anti-depressant industry busy.

A lanky resident ordered a Red-Eye, a favorite amongst those on call: coffee with four shots of espresso. Guaranteed to keep you awake when shit inevitably hit the fan on long, grueling shifts.

Dr. Ura—an ENT whose mother hadn't loved him enough—berated the barista: "I asked for three pumps of vanilla and this tastes like a two pumper, at best!" A vein pulsed his forehead, seen daily by terrorized scrub nurses, the general public—especially those in the service industry—and his wife Alice who was rumored to be fucking the lawn guy.

"Sorry about that, sir," the barista said, shooting Dr. Ura a dopey lopsided grin. His red eyes hinted at a puffed doobie before his shift, and he clearly didn't care a douchebag doctor was yelling at him which only served to infuriate Dr. Ura more.

"—having fun watching the show?" Wrenching my attention away from the two-pump vanilla altercation, I meet Aldea's gaze. A smirk haunted her lips.

"Oh yeah. Dr. Ura is about to blow a gasket," I answered.

Aldea took the seat across from me and watched Dr. Ura storm off; no doubt to call the CEO of The Coffee Bean to bitch about subpar service and blatant disrespect—to a doctor of all people. She pointed. "That guy? One of the worst humans I've ever had the displeasure to meet. Did you know he was in my med school class?"

"Jeez, no. What was that like?" I couldn't even imagine.

Aldea rolled her eyes. "He sat in the front row; reserved for ass kissers and douchebags. Before one anatomy exam, he bought every copy of the workbook from the bookstore so no one could study. The very definition of a gunner." She shrugged. "The only thing he's got going for him is he can fit comfortably in airplane seats.

Thankfully Shawn wasn't like that, short or a total dick. Of course... as of late, he hadn't been himself either. Remembering the red notebook, I cringed. "Right," I replied. I took another sip of my latte and gathered my thoughts. "So... what's going on?" I asked lamely.

When we'd hung out before, Aldea seemed bubbly and happy, but today she felt... off. Somewhat awkward. Stiff body language. Her jaw clenched periodically. She fidgeted, jittering her leg under the table, making her New Balance sneaker squeak against tile. Eyes flitted around the shop, lingering on the two medical students, then turning to me. "Oh, just your standard stuff. Spooky is doing well, running amuck without a limp." Her ruby lips stretched into a shy smile and the jittering stopped. Hard edges and angles melted away. "I'm going to ask Taylor to move in with me soon," she added.

"That's amazing! Shawn told me you were thinking about it."

Her cheeks pinked. "Yeah. I've never lived with a girlfriend before, so it'll be an adjustment. Thankfully Spooky loves her even if she was his vet."

"Have you ever been as serious about someone like this?" I asked.

Gazing at her hands, Aldea resumed fidgeting—twirling a rose gold ring on her thumb. "I mean... not really. Not that I haven't had girlfriends before but—" She paused. "My ex—well, she broke up with me shortly after Mom got sick. Said I didn't give her enough attention and she felt neglected," she added bitterly.

"Seriously?"

She nodded. "Yep. She got jealous of ALS. Can you believe it?"

"Unreal," I answered. So much for women being more understanding than men.

Aldea tapped her fingers on the table. "Listen—I wanted to talk to you about something."

Here it was: the pall cast over the entire meeting, the ulterior motive. Internal alarm bells sounded. "Okay..." I said. Her words had the same connotation of *we need to talk*, usually uttered before an unceremonious dumping or firing.

"It's not a huge deal but—" her eyes darted around the shop and satisfied no one was paying us any attention, she continued, "I know you were in my office after hours."

Oh shit. Oh shit. Oh shit.

Aldea gave me a wounded look. "What were you doing there? Why?"

I swallowed hard, hoping to lubricate my sandpaper throat with meager spit. "Well, I—uh—" I croaked. I tipped the cup to my lips and took a hearty swig. Better. "I guess... I was worried."

"Worried?" she asked. Her eyebrows steepled.

I fought the urge to squirm in my seat. "Yeah... about Shawn. About the chip."

Something flickered across her face, far too quick for me to register exactly what. Anger? Disappointment?

"What are you worried about?" she asked slowly.

I took a deep breath. *Just relax*, I told myself. *It's fine.* "It's just... Shawn seems, I dunno. *Different.* He's not himself. And I think you know what I mean."

Of course, Aldea knew: she'd written the same things in the notebook next to his name: *Fits of rage? Personality changes?*

On the surface, only little changes. He wasn't as quick to smile and didn't joke around like he used to. Not that he was wandering around totally morose, but an undercurrent of irritability radiated off him. He wasn't necessarily rude to me but his patience with me—once a wellspring—had become woefully thin. Snapping at me for the dumbest things; chewing too loud among them. Driving with him kept my nerves in a frazzled state.

Look at this stupid cocksucker, he said a few days ago, lip curling with contempt. Said cocksucker looked 80 years old with puffy silver hair poking above the driver's seat; egregiously traveling five miles under the speed limit. Shawn jammed on the gas pedal and motored past the unsuspecting grandma, shooting her a middle finger. At my look of horror, he'd replied, *What, babe? She pissed me the fuck off.*

Or he'd take something I said and twist it, reacting to a turn of phrase, picking fights over the dumbest things.

Aldea's eyes pinched shut and she let out a sigh, her shoulders slumping forward. She tilted her head and looked at me wearily. "I'll be honest with you Rachel. I'm worried too. There's been... incidences, stuff I haven't told you." Her hands spread in a *what are you gonna do?* gesture. "It's a little sticky since he's my patient; doctor/patient confidentiality and all that. I wanted to cut him a break; since he's also my friend." She extended a finger as if proving a point. "I checked Shawn's records, and he signed a release allowing me to pass medical information on to you. So *technically*, I'm not doing anything wrong by telling you this; just making that clear."

"Okay..."

"The first show we did with Brooke and Drake? When we went out to eat after, you left to pee and this guy at the bar stared at your ass and Shawn *flipped*. He got totally pissed off... I thought he was going to leap over the table and beat the dude's ass. It freaked me out," she said, picking at her ragged cuticles. "When you got back, he acted like nothing happened. I figured he must be the jealous type."

"I didn't remember thinking anything was off," I remarked. All in all, I thought we had a great time, in fact, remembered it as one of the last times Shawn was himself.

"Right. Then our last trip, when we went out to the club with his friend, Baylon?"

I rolled my eyes. "Don't get me started on Baylon; his only hobbies are women and illicit activities."

"Yeah... about that," she started. "Now mind you, I don't have definitive proof but at one point Shawn and Baylon disappeared and when they came back—Shawn had powder under his nose and was ... keyed up. Sweaty, wide eyed. You see it enough and it's easy to spot."

I knew what she meant. A career of taking care of patients on different drugs meant you saw how people were affected, how they acted. Meth? Tachycardic, often suffering from hallucinations and delusions, and freakish strength. Cocaine? Similar but less hallucinations; quick to anger. Nothing good came from either. Not that I was a prude—far from it. I enjoyed a few alcoholic beverages and smoking a joint on vacation but drew the line at hard stuff. Shawn mentioned a few wild nights on the road during his career, never going into the specifics and I was happy to keep it that way.

"I get it," I replied.

"They got a VIP booth—luckily, we didn't have people around us—and some guy grabbed me. I told him to let go. He didn't and Shawn warned him to stop—and he didn't so Shawn laid him out. Punched his lights out and finished with a nice swift kick to the ribs. And Rachel?" She gave me a searching look.

"What?" I asked.

Aldea shifted uncomfortably. "There was something in his eyes. A rage." Her brown eyes flicked down. "I wasn't sure he'd stop; it was like the light went out of his eyes. The—" she searched for the word. "The humanity, I guess?" Her fingernails found her forearm and she nervously scratched.

Unconsciously I rubbed my knuckles, remembering how he'd babied his hand. It all made sense.

"But then I got through to him and he was back; not intent on murdering some guy. He calmed down." Aldea leaned back in the chair. "Has he ever been like... that before? Quick to rage? Violent?"

I shook my head. "Never." A woman in blue scrubs scooted past our table, nearly toppling my drink; I reached out and steadied it.

Aldea paused, seemingly gathering her thoughts. "I mean—the whole road rage thing. How would you react if some redneck idiot screamed at you after rear-ending you? I'd be hard pressed not to punch the idiot's lights out too."

I leaned forward. "Aldea... he beat the absolute shit out of that guy, though. Pulverized him. That's so unlike Shawn. When he played basketball, he *never* got pulled into the on-court fights. Never even got a technical foul!" I added, "Once I walked in on him sobbing watching *The Notebook*." Now? I wondered if the story would affect him the same way.

I somehow doubted it.

"Side note: I love *The Notebook*. Great taste in movies," Aldea said.

"I mean... I guess?"

"*The Notebook* aside; I'm worried the chips might be... functioning *too well*. It's an inhibiting chip, right?" Aldea said.

"Right..."

Aldea continued, "I originally developed it for ALS, hoping to stimulate neurons but found it didn't work the way I'd hoped. After much research—trial and error—I realized it functioned more effectively as an *inhibitor*. It dampens and stops the signals causing headaches; stops 'em at the source."

"Okay..." I answered.

Aldea said, "What I'm getting at: in theory—it could inhibit other neurons too. Those responsible for mood and behavior." She tapped her fingers on the tabletop. "Have you ever heard about the University of Texas tower shooter?"

"Of course. I grew up in Austin," I answered. "Everyone knows about that."

She smacked her forehead. "That's right. Sorry, I forgot. Well, when they performed the autopsy on him, they found a tumor in his brain and thought it contributed to violent impulses. What if the chip's doing something like that? Inhibiting the pathways responsible for self-control. Instead of that voice in your head saying, *is that a good idea? Maybe I should rethink that?*—there's nothing. That little checkpoint is gone and Shawn's giving into his baser urges."

I knew what she meant. Waiting in line at the DMV was enough to incite homicidal urges from the best of us, but we contained it for the most part. "He's just reacting and unable to stop himself?" I asked.

She shrugged. "It's my working theory for now. It makes sense; explains other... cases too."

I let that slide. She could tell me later although I had a pretty good idea which cases she meant, and she knew it.

"But Rachel, I'm going to fix this, I promise you," Aldea said. "I thought you should know I'm worried too. I'm not mad at you for creeping around my office. I should have told you sooner."

I don't know if it was her earnest expression or kind words, but my anxiety receded—not completely but lessened. I answered, "Thank you."

"I'm going to do a functional MRI and see how Shawn's brain reacts. How it lights up."

I chuckled. "You're going to have to sedate him to high hell. He hates those things. Gets claustrophobic."

She smiled. "Funny you should say that; I need a favor."

33

Dr. Absinthe

Claire pulled me aside. "Aldea... we gotta do something."

"About what?" I asked, mind still on the earlier conversation with Rachel. "Shawn?"

She gave me a confused look. "What? No, Billie."

I groaned. "Oh God what happened now?" She'd seemed... okay enough recently. Still withdrawn and wan but hadn't assaulted any more patients.

Claire looked around—ensuring no one could eavesdrop—before continuing, "I got a phone call last night. From the police."

I muttered, "Been a lot of that lately."

"What?"

"Nothing. The police? Why?"

Claire's lips pressed into a thin line, and she exhaled loudly. "You remember how Billie and her boyfriend broke up? Or should I say: Billie's boyfriend broke up with *her*."

"Right."

"Well, she's been stalking him. Like *stalking* stalking," Claire said.

I repeated: "*Stalking* stalking?" I imagined Billie in all black with a baseball cap pulled low over her face following her ex at a distance, hiding behind brick walls and slinking about. Plucking his used tissues from trash cans and hugging them to her chest in a lonely bed. People went absolutely cuckoo after breakups sometimes.

Claire grimaced. "Like camping out at his apartment and waiting for him to get home from work. Following him when he leaves the house. Love letters. Gifts. The police told me at one point, she'd hand delivered a giant stuffed bear to his work, burst into a staff meeting, and started sobbing." Claire extended a finger. "And that's when Billie got slapped with the . You can't do that shit at people's work."

"A restraining order? Holy shit. That's... bad."

"Um yeah. Very bad. And per the police, Billie violated the restraining order; last night in fact."

"What did she do?" I asked, suddenly terrified of the answer. Hacked Jerry into tiny bits? Abducted him? And now that I thought about it; Billie wasn't at the receptionist's desk this morning—it was Georgia, one of our part-timers. Stomach acid bubbled and nausea washed over me. Images flashed within my mind: photos of Aubrey's splintered bone impaled in pale pink brains, clots of blood dotting its surface; Mrs. Reynolds' painful admission of her husband's sudden rage; whatever happened with Mrs. Combs and the bus; and Shawn.

"Last night, she followed Jerry... on a date. Followed them to the restaurant and—I don't know—I guess seeing them together set her off. Billie burst into the place, swept their wine glasses off the table, ranting, raving, screaming."

"Don't tell me she stabbed Jerry's date with a broken wine glass."

Claire tugged on her badge. "Nothing like that thankfully. Cops got there right away. But Billie was violating the restraining order so..." She mimed handcuffs slapping onto wrists. "Billie called me—she remembered my number and I bailed her out. She's home now, hopefully sleeping and not carving Jerry's initials into her skin or something."

I snapped my fingers. "Listen, can you call her and get here in here ASAP? I need to check some things out."

"What do you mean?" Claire asked.

I wondered how much to reveal and erred on the side of keeping my mouth shut. The less people that knew, the better. I already had a nurse clued in to the problem; best to keep Claire out of it. Sounded like Billie needed a functional MRI too.

"Just need to make sure nothing neurologic is going on. She has those migraines you know," I lied.

34

Shawn

M Y STOMACH RUMBLED, ECHOING off the waiting room walls. Aldea gave strict instructions to fast for the MRI if I wanted sedation and I sure as hell did. I'd suffered through too many MRIs and had PTSD from it; the tube closing in around me, suffocating me, time crawling by. Ugh. I couldn't stand it.

I clutched *Sports Illustrated*, pretending to read while surreptitiously watching the man across the room. He gripped a handheld game in one gnarled hand, a casino game based on the dinging slot noises. The other hand's index finger mined for gold; there were a lot of nose pickers amongst Aldea's patients. Each hand trembled, clearly in the grips of some terrible disease and I worried he was one violent jerk away from gouging his brain.

"Mr. Gilbert?"

Tearing my attention from the shaky nose picker currently examining his bounty with a greedy look—I stood up and made my way to the reception desk. Instead of Billie, it was a blandly pretty woman.

"Here," I said.

The woman gestured. "Dr. Absinthe is ready to see you now."

"Thanks."

Down the hallway I went past several shut doors. Reaching her office door, I knocked.

"Come in." Aldea said, voice muffled by wood.

I opened the door and did a double take. "Rachel? What are you doing here?"

She wore maroon scrubs with her hair pulled back in a loose ponytail. Standing up, she hugged me. Automatically, I wrapped my arms around her, still confused why she was here.

"I thought you had to work?" I asked.

Rachel shot me a big smile. "They called me off and Aldea said she needed some help."

"Help?" I asked.

Aldea cut in. "Claire got sick and unless I could get a nurse to help with your sedation for the MRI, we were going to have to cancel it." She laughed. "I figure you didn't want to have to fast again."

"You got that right," I answered.

Aldea shrugged. "I figured you'd be okay with it."

"It's whatever," I answered, tendrils of irritation licking through me. I clenched my jaw. "Let's get it over with." For some reason, seeing Rachel set me on edge.

But I couldn't quite say why.

35

Rachel

THIRTY MINUTES LATER, SHAWN was on the MRI table wearing a hideous hospital issued gown. An 18g IV rested in the crook of his arm—inserted by yours truly—and I hooked him to the cardiac monitor, ensuring all emergency supplies were readily within reach. I wasn't going to let *anything* happen to my husband; I only wanted to help him.

Shawn said, "Make sure you don't OD me, okay?"

"Don't tempt me," I joked.

Aldea called out from the other room: "You guys about ready?" The MRI tech stood next to her, roped into our little don't-let-anyone-know-what-we're-doing-scam: part two. Part one happened last night with Billie—Aldea's receptionist and chip recipient—also displaying erratic behavior. Aldea secured the MRI tech's silence with the promise of a great letter of rec for medical school.

"Yeah," I called out. Turning to Shawn, I said, "Have a nice MRI."

He curtly nodded and shut his eyes.

I injected ten cc's of Versed into his IV and watched tension melt from his face. His heart rate decreased, and his breathing slowed—not enough for me to be concerned. "Shawn?" I asked.

"Hmmmm?" he asked dreamingly.

"Wiggle your fingers for me," I said, and he complied, waggling them lazily. Appropriate sedation—relaxed but able to interact and respond.

The table began to move, and Shawn inched up the tube. It clanged, making me grit my teeth. No wonder people wanted doped up to get these things. Another thing that sucks about MRIs? They take *forever*. A CT scan takes only minutes; it takes longer to transfer the patient and get them situated than it does for the study most of the time.

While the machine whirred—taking its sweet time reconstructing Shawn's anatomy—I worried. What if something *was* wrong? What if he was brain damaged from this? Could Aldea... could *we* fix it? Another scary thought occurred to me: what if it wasn't the chip at all? Maybe my husband had changed, becoming someone I sometimes didn't recognize. Or maybe... it was something else entirely, completely unrelated. He'd taken his fair share of knocks to the head, resulting in few concussions. Not as much as a football player or a boxer but enough—especially the last head injury; the BIG one. *Chronic traumatic encephalopathy* they called it; Will Smith starred in a movie about it. Athletes lost their shit, killing their entire family or taking their own lives. It was all over the news.

Aldea's tinny voice instructed, "Shawn. Think of something happy." A faint smile stretched Shawn's lips. "Perfect. Wiggle your toes." He did. "Great! Now Shawn—" she stopped. "I'm going to ask you to think about that man that rear-ended you." Shawn's fists curled and his eyebrows steepled. "Think about how he damaged your car, how he acted," she said. Shawn's body tensed and I caught Aldea's eyes. She shook her head and mouthed: *pissed*. "Enough of that. Think about the waves breaking on an ocean. Bask."

Aldea mimed depressing a syringe and I injected him with two cc's of Versed; helping him maintain calm. Leaving the MRI tech's side, Aldea came up to me and in a low voice said, "His amygdala and hypothalamus are lighting up like a Christmas tree. They're the parts responsible for anger," she explained. "More than I would expect of the average person; like how violent offenders' brains react. Since Shawn can't consent right now—being that he's nice and sedated—are you okay with me dialing the settings back? Then we'll see how his brain reacts."

My heart fluttered. We had to try something, but I still felt uneasy about the whole thing. "Go ahead. We need to see what happens," I replied.

Back she went to the small alcove. Her laptop opened. I checked on Shawn again: vitals stable, still nice, and relaxed.

Aldea called out, "Okay, I adjusted the settings. Let's see what happens now." MRI clanged and Aldea said, "Shawn. Purse your lips and stick out your tongue." With a sleepy giggle, Shawn did. "Think about that guy at the restaurant, the one that stared at Rachel's ass. Remember how he looked at her?" Aldea asked. Shawn's fingers tensed, then relaxed. "What about that asshole at the club that grabbed me?"

Not even a flicker of movement and his heart rate stayed a cool fifty.

Aldea shot me a thumb up and mouthed: *better.*

It went on like this until Aldea proclaimed the chip "reprogramed" and terminated the study. As Shawn recovered Aldea remarked, "Both Shawn and Billie's brain lit up in the same areas; those responsible for anger and impulse control." She tapped her forehead. "Frontal lobe, amygdala, and hypothalamus. After dialing back the settings those areas still lit up, but it's more like flickers, not an atomic bomb explosion."

"How do we know it's going to work?" I asked.

Aldea winced. "We don't. But we can hope. At least we're doing *something*, trying to fix the issue, and it's gotta mean something that the reaction was far less than the previous settings."

"I guess that's a win," I replied.

Aldea put her hand on my forearm. "Listen... if you think anything is off... let me know, okay? We're all in this together and we'll fix it. I promise."

She gave my arm a reassuring squeeze which helped assuage my nerves.

Some.

36

Dr. Absinthe

"HEY BABE, YOU DOIN' okay?" Taylor said.

I jerked my head up. "What?"

Pointing with her fork—a limp piece of broccoli clinging to the tines—she said, "You haven't touched your food."

"That's not true," I argued, knowing she was right; more like pushing my food around the plate. Relocating chicken south. Broccoli north. Occasionally prodding lettuce soaked with balsamic vinaigrette. To prove my point, I speared a piece of chicken and placed it in my mouth. "See? Yum!" It wasn't. It was dry and minimally seasoned, but Taylor worked hard on it and who was I to turn my nose up at a home cooked meal? It was the thought that counted anyway.

Taylor asked, "What's bothering you? You've been all out of sorts tonight."

I chuckled. "Am I that obvious?"

Her lip curled. "I just know you, Aldea. Now spill: what's the problem?"

A black furry paw tapped my left thigh, claws at the ready. Spooky lived for chickee night. I dropped a piece on the floor for him; someone might as well enjoy it. "Well... it's Shawn's chip."

"What's wrong with it?"

I shrugged. "I think his chip was working too well. It was inhibiting far more than the impulses responsible for his migraines. Rachel and I noticed—" I stopped and glanced at Taylor, ticking them off on my fingers as I spoke, "Anger. Rage. Impulse control."

Taylor nodded. "I remember you telling me about the guy at the club, but it sounded like he had it coming, honestly. Grabbing you like that?" Her dark eyes flashed. "I would've punched his lights out too."

"My knight in shining armor," I joked. "Well… I told Rachel my concerns." I conveniently left out the part where I busted Rachel creeping around my office in the middle of the night. "We performed a functional MRI yesterday and when I adjusted the chip's settings, his anger decreased. So, it seems kind of damning… like the chip was at fault. But I fixed it. I think." I sipped the red wine Taylor set out with dinner, allowing oaky tones to wash over my tongue. "Thanks for listening to me vent. It's nice to be able to confide in someone instead of being left alone with my thoughts running wild."

"That's what girlfriends do! Of course. I'm sure it'll all be fine," Taylor said.

"Sure," I said, unconvincingly.

"Trust me babe," she said, shooting me an impish grin. "I'm a doctor."

I had to give her that. "That's true. But so am I."

"My hot doctor. My McDreamy," Taylor said, batting her eyes.

"Oh, stop it." I said, hoping she'd do nothing of the sort. Taylor leaned over and kissed my forehead. Her eucalyptus shampoo clung to her hair and its scent washed over me, making me think of home.

Taylor. Taylor was home.

"Move in with me?" I asked. The question bubbled right out, spurred on by the heat swirling in my chest. Heart jackrabbited against sternum.

Taylor squealed and stomped her feet. "Aldea, are you serious? Not joking around with me, right? My little heart couldn't take it." She looked radiant.

I shook my head. "Not joking one bit. Come live with me. And Spooky," I added.

"At the risk of being one of those U-Hauling lesbians, I gratefully accept," she said. Her eyes were far too bright, hinting at tears of happiness threatening to overspill her lids. Surprising me, she scooped me up in her arms as if I weighed nothing more than a ragdoll.

"Oh wow. I love a good set of muscles. Where is the strong woman taking me?" I asked coquettishly.

Her wicked grin resurfaced, and my blood roared. "To bed," she answered.

Sometime between Taylor stripping my clothes off and kissing down my body—lingering at the parts that drove me crazy: the hollow of my neck, just above my navel, and sensitive inner thighs—and the multiple orgasms, Rachel texted.

And when I finally saw her text—Come over, something's wrong—I reacted, throwing my clothes on, and I raced over to their apartment.

By the time I arrived—

It was too late.

37

Shawn

T HE CRAWL OF TRAFFIC didn't bother me for once; maybe the sedation for the MRI yesterday reset my mood or something. It helped that every song on the local radio station's playlist was a banger. I sung lyrics thought long forgotten, drudging them up from a file cabinet deep within my psyche. Whistling—keeping the party vibe going—I unlocked the door, barely crossing the threshold when my phone rang. Scanning the screen, I groaned.

My lawyer.

Lawyers never called to check in or just shoot the shit. If she was calling... it wasn't good. I steeled my nerves and answered, "Hello?"

"Shawn, it's Cheryl," she said in her thick New York accent.

I gritted my teeth. "I know. Hi," I said flatly.

A pregnant pause.

"Have a moment to talk?"

I removed my sneakers and flopped down on the couch. Did I have a moment? Yes. Did I want to give away my moment to Cheryl? No. She billed by the minute too. "I guess," I answered.

Cheryl cleared her throat; a phlegmy rattle that spoke to a pack-a-day smoking habit, and asked, "Does the name, Brynn Matthews ring a bell to you?"

I stopped breathing. "Who?" I rasped, my mouth a sudden desert.

"Brynn Matthews," Cheryl repeated.

Heat licked up my back, filling my chest cavity with fire. And fear. Stalling, I said, "Umm..." Did I remember Brynn Matthews? It was hard to forget her; but time helped. Things spectacularly crumbled to shit with us in the end. I thought of her auburn hair fanning across my bare chest in bed, those striking emerald eyes; sultry and smoldering, and a pair of pouty lips that felt amazing wrapped around me. Oh shit. "No. Should it?" I lied, striving for a carefree tone.

Cheryl let out a rueful laugh. "That's the question of the hour, isn't it?" Her voice hardened, becoming all business with sharp consonants. "This *Brynn Matthews*—" Cheryl said it haughtily, the same way she'd say the word *allegedly* in court "—has been hitting up gossip rags: US *Weekly*, TMZ, and... she's been talking about *you*."

Panic flooded my body, starting at the crown of my head and cascading down. As the years passed, I'd put it all out of my mind; allowing my anxiety to relax and occasionally, even hibernate. Sure, sometimes fear reared its ugly head, but it was easy enough to stamp down. A false sense of security—of complacency—settled over me. *That's just the past,* I'd reason. *Nothing to worry about.* But here it was: the skeleton in my closet. What else could it be?

"Me? Why?" I asked, holding out a desperate hope it wasn't what I thought.

Cheryl proceeded to shatter my world: "This is the bad part. Very bad. This *Brynn Matthews* is saying you got her pregnant during your championship season and paid for her to get an abortion. Plus—" Cheryl hissed. "She's saying you gave her hush money if she didn't go public with it."

"WHAT?" I shouted. My jaw clenched and my teeth gnashed together. Fuck. Fuck. Fuck.

Cheryl sighed. "Yeah, told you it was bad. Now listen Shawn, I'm going to ask you once, and only once: is this true?"

"I—it—uh—" I sputtered.

She cut me off, "As your lawyer, I can only help if you tell me the truth. If she's full of shit, we'll sue the pants off her for libel. Make her regret ever opening her dirty mouth."

I pinched the bridge of my nose and lied: "No, it's not true." Even to my ears, it sounded like a filthy fucking farce. My skin tightened and I waited for Cheryl to call me on my bullshit.

"Okay," Cheryl said. "Don't talk to the press if they approach you and don't worry—they will. Those scum buckets from TMZ will hang from your skylight if you let them. Stay inside. I'm going to coordinate with your publicist and release a statement soon. I'll run it past you first, don't worry," she rasped.

"Uh, thanks," I said dumbly. I wrapped my hand around my neck and squeezed; the anxiety invading my muscles, knotting them, and pulling them tight. My fingers grazed the back of my head and I recoiled at the heat; fingertips singed as if I'd touched a hot stove. I put the abused fingers in my mouth with a wince. Other than the fiery burn at the base of my neck, my body felt horribly numb; a tooth deadened by Novocain.

"And seriously, don't answer the door," Cheryl said, and the line clicked. Not big on goodbyes or niceties that one. Dead air filled my ear, a low hum my skull. Part of me felt completely detached from my body, as if I was a mere onlooker during the conversation that would dismantle my life, my marriage. But below that numb feeling was a molten core that bubbled and roiled, just dying to rage, and let it out. Punch, hit, kick, bite, whatever.

I took a deep inhale in and let loose: "FUCK!" Every desensitized nerve ending roared to life, amplifying each emotion exponentially. I crumpled to my knees and thrust my face into my hands. Tears—steaming hot—cut a path down my cheeks. Sobs racked my body while dual emotions warred within me: Sorrow. Deep, repentant sorrow. Etched into each muscle fiber.

And—

Anger.

I wanted to grab Brynn Matthews and rip that head of auburn hair right off her neck, fucking decapitate her. Peer at her neck bones with my own two eyes, examining ruined blood vessels spurting blood. Shake her until she screamed; begged for me to stop. Ruin her life like she was ruining mine. Even if the story was true—every bit of it—I didn't deserve this! Through a miracle of modern technology, I reclaimed my life and was finally *living*.

Then this.

Another sob shook me. Oh God. How was I going to break this to Rachel? I'd already lied to her, remembering our conversation clear as day even though it took place years ago on one of our dates.

Rachel took a bite of an artisan pretzel smothered with cheese. "Gonna toss you a hardball right now, Mr. Gilbert," she said with a mischievous glint in her eye.

"Shoot," I replied. "And my rebound record was nothing to sneeze at, just to be clear."

Pointing with the pretzel—jagged from her nibbles—she asked, "Have you ever gotten a woman pregnant?"

I'd choked on my drink then, sputtering and hacking. Luckily, it bought me time to craft my response. I violently cleared my throat and hit my chest with a closed fist. Coughed. With a faint wheeze, I replied, "Sorry. Wrong pipe."

"Don't worry, I was monitoring you closely for signs of choking." Rachel waved her hand. "And just because you nearly died doesn't mean you get out of answering the question."

I laughed—it came out tinny and canned to my ears. "Wouldn't dream of it." I forced myself to look into her eyes and reached across the table, grasping her hands. My pulse thumped in my ears—faster and faster. "Never," I answered, quickly adding, "At least... as far as I know." Tossed in at the last second, just in case.

Still... Rachel would know I lied. Lied massively. Lied right to her face.

My breath caught. She might *already* know. The tabloids could have already broken the news; I couldn't bear to search my name online, terrified of what I might find. And if she didn't know, one of her gossipy coworkers would let her—or everyone *but* her—know.

"Fuck, fuck, FUCK!" I yelled, my voice echoing in our small apartment. Red overtook my vision. I screamed until I tasted blood, and my vocal cords were shredded.

This must be what it feels like to lose your mind.

38

Rachel

E VERY PART OF MY body ached. According to my watch I'd traveled 18,000 steps and my morning jog only contributed 5,000 of those. My arches throbbed, a tired sort of electricity zapping the strength from my calves and shins. Jelly legs. Today's shift belonged in a special circle in Hell, one I hadn't yet descended to despite plenty of horrific shifts.

All thanks to a tampered drug. Spice. K2. Another hazard of my job was becoming intimately familiar with underground elements: to take care of my patients, I had to understand what fucked up shit they were using or doing. I learned all the slang names too: Blaze, Demon (a rather telling name for how folks acted on the stuff), Crazy Clown, Fire (fitting since the ER went down in flames as the shift progressed), way too many to count. Whatever you called it, it was a synthetic marijuana, touted to be THC free so you could pass a pesky drug test but *still* get high. And some idiot—whether intentionally or stupidly—laced the stuff with brodifacoum: a rather devastating rat poison that causes creatures to bleed from every orifice and internally.

And it didn't affect only rats this time.

The first patient showed up at about eight.

"Nurse to the front!" came a panicked voice from the overhead speakers. The beginning of a scream echoed, abruptly cut off when registration hung up. Screams were never good. Two nurses hurried out the double doors to more screams.

We all glanced at each other wearily, slowly pulling on gloves because we knew whatever was happening was going to be bananas.

"Get me a bed! Now!" Steve yelled, pushing a slumped over man in a wheelchair. Then the guy moaned and puked up a fountain of blood. Looked at us with sanguine eyes. *Subconjunctival hemorrhages*: broken vessels in the whites of his eyes, staining them crimson. Huge clots dribbled out both nostrils. He grimaced, displaying rusty teeth lined with dark maroon grout.

"Oh shit," I said. A phrase I came to repeat many times over during the shift, intermittently punctuating it with a *what in the actual fuck?*

He was only the first patient. In a matter of hours every bed was filled with patients hemorrhaging. For some, it was their bowels—causing toilet to look like crime scenes. Other with gross hematuria: peeing straight blood, sometimes unable to void large clots that lodged in the urethra, necessitating a catheter which caused a whole slew of other problems. Intracranial hemorrhages; white starbursts decorating head CTs. Minor traumas meant massive intra-abdominal hemorrhages. We ran out of blood in the first few hours and chewed through every reversal agent we could think of, throwing the pharmaceutical kitchen sink at them. All because some idiot wanted to poison people, causing them to bleed out; or they thought rat poison would lead to a killer high.

Worst shift of my life. Maybe I should ask Aldea if she was hiring... helping with the functional MRI and the sedation was a breeze compared to today.

Pure exhaustion filled me and only determination to reach a hot shower powered my legs. Staggering into the apartment my back tightened, almost going into a spasm—and I took a sharp inhalation, staving off the cramp... barely. "Ooof," I moaned, grabbing the small of my back. Even through the pain, I heard the hollow quality of my voice and realized something felt... off. It was quiet of the worst kind. Unexpected. Echoing. Most nights the TV blared; tuned to ESPN or sometimes MTV for the rare times they actually played music videos. Shawn liked having background noise. A life of migraines left him with an intolerance of anything excessive—auditory or visual—leaving him to stew in silence, in the dark, in pain. Him having background noise was further proof the chip was working for his migraines.

But the other stuff... No, Aldea fixed it. I watched her do it.

"Hello?" I called out, feeling a bit like an idiot in a horror flick, announcing my presence to the still-lurking killer.

Silence met me. Not even the sounds of distant activity; putzing around the bedroom, the flushing of the toilet, a microwave dinging. It felt empty... but empty wasn't the right word. Not even close. It felt like a desolate nothing and *nothing* was worse than *something*. The mind took nothing and transformed it, dreaming up horrific scenarios: an intruder, a rapist, discovering Shawn dead in a pool of blood—I'd seen so much of it today and couldn't get it out of my head. And per Aldea, Shawn wasn't totally averse to imbibing certain illicit substances these days although K2 was a stretch, even for him.

"Shawn?" I called out again. My skin crawled, prickling underneath my scrub sleeves but a cold sweat bloomed in my armpits. Stagnant air hung about—not even the hint of air conditioning kicking on or a breeze from a cracked window. Dead air. Wrong. I put my purse on the entryway table—where most things went: keys, mail, loose change, and it skidded loudly, sending my heart into my throat. So loud. Too loud in the *nothing*.

"Are you here?" I asked, keeping my voice low.

Shucking my work Crocs, I changed into my house shoes and padded down the hallway. Each footfall larger than life, further highlighting my solitude. I struggled to slow my breathing, cognizant gulping air would drive my heart rate up, putting me in fight or flight mode; triggering my body to freak out, practically begging for a panic attack or hysterics.

Calm down, Rachel. Not a big deal. Shawn just stepped out. Or he's taking a shit. Chill.

Leaning forward, I peered into our bedroom. "Shawn?"

Shadows inhabited the room, giving mean edges to the furniture—pointed and frightening—whispering untold horrors. Only one way to fix that: light chased the dark away. Light would bring everything into stark perspective. My hand wavered at the light switch; a quick flick of the wrist up, that's all it took. Fingers trembled and quivered, evident even in the muddy dark.

Did I want to see? What would I see? Was I freaking myself out for nothing? I didn't want to see:

I had to.

Pushing air forcefully from my lungs, I flipped the light switch and bathed the room in vibrant yellow. Hard angles softened, becoming a harmless dresser strewn with folded clothing, a laundry hamper in the corner, and—

A low moan came from the bathroom. Or... had I imagined it? I paused. Each muscle stiffened. "Shawn?" I croaked.

The illumination overhead didn't extend to the master bathroom; one of the largest rooms in the apartment. His and Hers sinks. A tub large enough for me to lounge in and read books but poor Shawn could barely contort his long frame into it. A shared toilet.

I crept towards the bathroom door, frantically looking around the room. The fine hairs at the nape of my neck were painfully tight and when I felt like this; I heeded the warning. Intuition. I'd seen enough movies to know being unprepared was a death sentence and my mother didn't raise an idiot. I spied Shawn's NBA Championship ring on the nightstand and dashed forward, snatching it up and slipping it on my finger, liking the heft of it. It wasn't brass knuckles, but it would do. The cool metal against my fingers calmed me somewhat, lending me some outside comfort however meager.

I tiptoed and paused just outside the bathroom doorframe. Feeling foolish—especially if the light snapped on to nothing of note—but better safe than sorry. If no one was there; no one could see me looking stupid I reasoned. I groped for the light, unwilling to expose the rest of my body until I saw what awaited me. If anything. Maybe I'd gotten into my own head, too much stress and too little sleep, my imagination running away with me.

I flicked the light switch up. and peered around the door frame.

And I saw Shawn.

His back was flush against the tub and his head drooped forward. Hair normally coiffed to perfection hung down; the ends soaking wet. Beads of perspiration rolled down his face.

"Shawn?" I whispered, grasping his forearms, and gently squeezing. With my index and middle finger, I found his radial pulse. Tried to count and lost it. Tachycardic, in the 140s at least. He had a heartbeat; albeit a fast one for whatever reason. Unbidden, Shawn's functional MRI popped into my head: swathes of color uptake—far too much—in the amygdala and frontal lobes. Angry reds, brilliant blues, fiery yellows, Aldea pointed them all out with regret in her eyes. So much activity lay underneath the surface, unseen to the naked eye but seen through the lens of science.

Did something go wrong? I wondered.

He let out another low moan, lips barely twitching. Long eyelashes brushed against flushed cheeks; fluttered but didn't open. The line between his eyes wrinkled then ironed itself out.

Could he even feel me touching him? I thought not, suspecting he hovered somewhere between unconscious and dazed. Satisfied with his breathing, I examined the rest of him. Shirtless torso showed off hard-earned gym muscles, skin glowing with a sheen of sweat. Finding no injuries there, I moved on. Noggin seemed fine, ditto his outstretched legs. He wore only a pair of boxer briefs—patterned with absurd pink flamingos. His skin was blazing hot. He needed a towel soaked with cold water. I should check his temperature.

I stood and before I could even take a step, Shawn's left hand clamped around my ankle with startling speed and strength. My chest seized and a shrill voice screeched in my head: TOLD YOU SOMETHING WAS WRONG! and I fought an intense urge to kick out, a hysterical urge to react. Unholy heat radiated from his palm and fingers, scorching my skin. I glanced down—feeling and hearing the tendons layered throughout my neck creaking—and saw Shawn's face. His lips were pulled back in a sneer, exposing a brutal grin too big for his face. Unnatural. Jaw muscles clenched powerfully, and manic eyes rolled like a sick pig hearing the screams of slaughter from its brethren. Sweat slicked his forehead, reflecting the fluorescent lights from the vanity.

A faint whimper escaped my lips and I fought to keep my teeth from chattering.

Shawn's rictus grin widened, and his gaze alighted on me. He giggled and said:

"Babe, we need to talk."

39

Shawn

RACHEL GAPED AT ME; a stupid, infuriating expression on her face. Fear widened her eyes, showing off too much white. Dark pupils found me, and her eyebrows arched. Her leg shook underneath my grip, a quivering livewire; *what the fuck was her problem?*

The rest of bathroom came into view.

How had I ended up here?

At first there was nothing then a sinister whisper supplied: *Brynn Matthews. Remember? Your sort-of-girlfriend that you forced to get an abortion and paid off. That ol' bug came back and bit you square in the ass.*

Bile rose in my throat and my annoyance with Rachel's face deepened to anger's perverse cousin: shame; a green, sickly emotion that made everything within me curdle and sour. Why didn't I just tell Rachel the truth when she asked? Knowing her like I do now, I doubt she would have judged. *She would have judged if she knew what you did. How you handled it,* my mind supplied.

My hand tightened around her ankle, fingers digging into her scrubs and flesh.

"Shawn," she said, her tone even. "Let me go, please." Her head tilted and I followed its movement, surprised at how tight my grip was; I didn't realize my own strength.

I let go and before Rachel drew away, I caught a glimpse of her skin: reddened with hints of purple. I'd grabbed her *hard*. More transgressions to feed the deadly shame spiral swirling within me—shoveling in a steady fuel of indignant anger and something that felt dangerously like not giving a shit about the consequences to words or actions.

I watched Rachel move around the bathroom. She stopped at the medicine cabinet and rummaged—for what? Something for me? Remembering her expression; the mistrust, I wondered: *Something to use against me?*

Bottles clinked together. "What's going on Shawn?" Rachel asked, still picking through the cabinet. She sounded irritated... but why? At finding me like this on the floor... and *why* was I on the bathroom floor to begin with? A black hole of nothing greeted me. Did she know? Was she waiting for me to confess, beg for forgiveness?

I scrutinized her for a clue. "What?" I said stupidly.

I heard a faint *whoosh*: Rachel sending a text. Wait... Who was she texting? The green-eyed monster reached into my chest and grasped my heart in its filthy grip.

Hands full, she closed the cabinet door and gave me a searching glance. "Seriously?"

"What?" I repeated. Impatience crept in—why was she acting so sketchy? "What are you talking about?"

Rachel rolled her eyes and my impatience morphed, growing teeth. I couldn't stand when she did that; hated it. Without speaking, Rachel conveyed: *You stupid asshole.*

"Don't play dumb with me," she said, busying herself with supplies in her hand.

I glared at her, stared down at my hands, then back to Rachel's face. Her expression softened. "Shawn, I'm not mad, just worried. Tell me: what's wrong?"

Brynn Matthews: that was what was wrong. Everything came crashing back and a sour gorge rose in my throat. That cunt. As if it were yesterday, Brynn's face stamped itself in my mind; those inviting eyes and that playful smirk. *I'm a dancer*, she said. And not at some second-rate strip club where most of the strippers had stretch marks and c-section scars. No, a backup dancer for some big names, most of which I'd recognized. Brynn had seemed *different*. Not overly impressed with me being a ball player and like an idiot, I'd fallen for her act—hook, line, and sinker. *You don't need to wear a condom, I'm on birth control*, she'd remarked from her position on the bed on hands and knees, nude save for a G-string that left nothing to the imagination. I'd been only too happy to throw caution to the wind. Again. And again. I'd been such a fucking idiot. I swallowed hard and clenched my jaw, desperately trying to suppress the rage bubbling within. Pressure—so much pressure—building, filling every cell in me, just begging to explode.

Rachel bent over me. Her gentle fingers wrapped around my right hand and squeezed. Worry colored her face. "Are you okay?"

"No, I'm fucking not," I snapped. "You'd know that if you paid any attention."

Displeasure flashed. "Well... then tell me what the fucking problem is," Rachel said in a snarky tone. "I'm not a mind reader." Rachel's annoyance piled on my shitty night and just like that—the dam burst.

"Goddammit!" I screamed and made to yank my hand from hers. Almost as if she'd expected my reaction, she held on firmly and pulled me back. The germ of anger proliferated with stunning speed, spreading throughout my entire body and I reacted without thought. My left hand shot up and roared through the air.

SMACK!

I slapped my wife. Her soft skin instantly reddened, and she let out a sharp cry. Startled eyes found mine and the look of supreme hurt nearly broke up my heart. *What had I done?*

But it was too late. My surroundings wavered around me, the bathroom tinted in crimson tones, and my consciousness ebbed and bled away from me. A pure, euphoric rage guided me and the wounded, terrified look on Rachel's face fed it.

Everything went black.

40

Rachel

I REELED FROM THE slap, my head rocking back. My cheek stung and I didn't doubt Shawn left a handprint there, if not a faint bruise come tomorrow.

Shock washed over me. I thrust my hand up to my face, cool fingertips stroking the raised skin and my mind raced. Had this really happened?

My husband slapped me.

He slapped me. He slapped me. He slapped me. Over and over, it repeated. He'd never so much as raised a hand to me. Hadn't ever even shouted at me until recently.

Only after the chip.

"What—?" I started but the words died in my mouth. Moving with startling speed, Shawn got to his feet and in the matter of seconds, towered over me. His fists clenched. Unclenched. Eyes flashed, wide and bright but without any semblance of humanity behind them. He looked... unhinged. "Shawn?" I said, my voice breaking.

He sneered. "You fucking bitch," he said, spitting the insult like venom. Pure venom. Even though I looked up into my husband's face—a face I'd seen hundreds of times a day for years—I recognized no part of him. Anger twisted his features, rendering him a monster; like a demon had gotten ahold of a Shawn Gilbert mask and thrust it over its face. It was him but... it wasn't. I had the impression of candlewax melting, distorting everything I once knew and loved: strong jaw, long eyelashes, the smile that made my stomach clench.

I put my hands up to protect myself and remembered: the ring. Gold and diamonds glittered, a massive thing.

It was my only chance to do some damage.

Roaring, I leapt at him. His face twisted in surprise and his mouth gaped open; too stunned to react. My left hand raked across his eyes, and he screamed, grabbing his face. His skin bunched underneath my fingernails. Heart pounding, I punched with my right hand—ring perched on my middle finger—and it collided with his mouth. I heard and felt teeth break underneath my grip and several sharp fragments cut my knuckles. But I didn't stop there. Again and again, I lashed out. Nose shattered. I opened skin above his left eye and blood ran down from a jagged laceration, obscuring his vision. He wrenched his head away and without a target, I punched again, colliding with his occiput, cutting open the scar from his chip.

He stumbled to his knees and screamed, "You dumb fucking cunt!"

Reacting almost on instinct, I reached into my pocket and pulled my phone out. My hand shook with adrenaline, and I barely got my thumbprint to read. The screen unlocked, showing my text message to Aldea:

> Come over, something's wrong.

Knowing time was short, instead of calling 911 which might waste precious seconds I didn't have, I tapped Aldea's name, and it started dialing.

"Oh no you don't!" Shawn yelled, ripping the phone away before I could see if it connected or if she'd answered. His voice was wet with blood and snot, twisted with rage. Without another look, he flung it away and phone collided with mirror.

Crack!

The mirror splintered and broke. Shards cascaded to the floor—some miniscule, no more than flecks of sharp dust while others were large enough to embed themselves deep within skin and sinew—rained down. I screamed and cowered, covering my head with my arms. Glass bit my forearms. I barely had time to register the insult because Shawn threaded his fingers through my hair and forcibly yanked me up. I heard hair follicles tearing from their nests and my scalp shrieked yet up I went. Immense pain sounded but nothing compared to the ache in my heart. "S—Shawn—please... please stop," I begged.

He merely leered at me through a mask of blood and fury and flung me aside just as he had with my phone. I collided with the wall, my head smacking into—then through—drywall. Stars dominated my entire visual field. Inky black invaded my periphery and the stars coalesced, turning everything a dishwater gray. I felt my grip on reality loosening. Right before I succumbed to blissful unconsciousness, I heard him:

Shawn, laughing with maniacal glee.

My stomach flip-flopped and certainty rose within me. I was going to die. My husband was going to kill me.

Then I melted into the ether.

41

Dr. Absinthe

I RACED TO THE Gilberts' apartment, running stop signs, and stamping on the gas pedal when traffic lights went yellow, flying through a few reds accompanied by the sound of blaring horns. The BPM channel on Sirius XM played; the fast tempo only serving to heighten my anxiety and I turned the volume down until the music became a mere whisper.

> Come over, something's wrong.

I thought of the text again and worried.

Shawn.

It could only mean something was wrong with Shawn. Had I fucked up? By adjusting his settings, had I made things worse?

Another car honked at me, bringing me out of my thoughts and I swerved, barely missing the Tesla. The driver gave me a middle finger salute and yelled out the window: "Stupid bitch! Watch where you're going!"

Normally such a reaction would have triggered my own road rage, but my anxiety was too high. Traversing the last few blocks, I pulled into an open spot in front of their apartment complex and killed the engine. Staring at their building—where I suspected their unit was—I saw nothing amiss. Blazing yellow light. No silhouettes throttling the shit out of their wife. I spotted my metal reflex hammer on the passenger seat—a gift from my mother—and grabbed it on impulse. The phrase: *Like bringing a knife to a gun fight* occurred to me but hell, it was better than nothing.

Unlike the dinky plastic hammers some folks used, my hammer had a little heft to it and could cause some damage. Extricating myself from the front seat, I shut the door and locked it with my remote. Clenching the cool hammer in sweaty hands, I ran through the lobby door and bolted up the stairs. One, two, three flights, and I was on their floor, panting with the exertion. Down their hall I went, and reaching their door, I found it ajar. Alarm bells rung in my head, and I swallowed painfully. When watching horror movies, this was the part where I always thought *call the police, you idiot* but here I was, about to commit idiocy. But I couldn't call for help; I had to see what was going on before involving anyone else.

Cautiously, I pushed the door open, cringing when it creaked. No one came running.

I entered the apartment into the living room. Clear.

My fingers wrapped around my reflex hammer. Should I head to the kitchen? Grab a butcher knife? I quickly vetoed the idea. Shawn was a big dude, and it would be child's play to wrest a knife from me and turn it against me... if it came to that.

Coming upon another room, I peered inward: the bedroom. Lights blazed and though the bedroom looked orderly enough, the adjacent master bath looked a mess. Toiletries and cosmetics littered the floor, and an overwhelming reek of perfume wafted my way. I wrinkled my nose.

"What are you doing here?"

I jumped and whirled around. "Oh!" I exclaimed.

Shawn.

"I said: what are you doing here?" he asked. His words slurred together as if he were drunk—or maybe it was all the fractured teeth poking out of bloodied gums; bottom lip split like engorged fruit. His nose canted to the right, obviously broken, and wounds decorated his face, each copiously bleeding. Someone kicked the shit out of him. He glared at me through one good eye—the other's surrounding skin was purpled and raw, open a mere slit.

"Uh... hi, S—Shawn," I stammered, taking a step back.

He grunted and brought his hand up to his face and gingerly touched his eye. Swollen knuckles stared back at me, and dried blood clung to his skin, caked in the wrinkles. I expected him to surge forward and grab me, pummel me to death but he appeared dazed; there was no way he didn't have a massive concussion.

Gazing into the bathroom, I saw a single Croc—woman's sized—streaked with blood. "Um... Shawn... where's Rachel?" I asked, certain I knew the answer. If he heard my question, he gave no indication nor answer, only continued rubbing his face as if trying to soothe himself. Blood splattered his chest, clinging to the whorls of dark hair. Keeping my eyes trained on him, I slowly backed towards the bathroom. One step. Two. What I was doing was incredibly stupid: backing into a corner without means of escape, but I didn't know what else to do.

I had to check on Rachel.

Bloody Croc became inert leg.

Chanced another glance at Shawn. He'd shut his good eye and groaned, grabbing his forehead. "My fucking head."

I continued. Another leg, torso, limbs, and—

I gasped at Rachel's poor face.

Shawn forgotten for the moment, I rushed to Rachel and kneeled next to her. Pressing my fingers to her neck, I felt a rush of relief on feeling a pulse—weak but there. She took a sonorous breath and her mouth flopped open. Most of her teeth were fractured at the gumline, white nubs poking through ravaged gums, reminding me of broken headstones in a graveyard. Her formerly delicate nose revealed a nasal bridge swollen to twice its size. A massive contusion overtook her right eye, swelling it completely shut, so like her husband's. A multitude of bruises littered her face: a purple thundercloud on her cheek, bluish blotches on her forehead. I followed the curve of her forehead and found a nasty laceration buried in the hairline. Creamy galea peeked out and I cringed seeing the tough fibrous connective tissue—if she'd been hit with more force, I could expect to see her skull. As I watched, Rachel's non-battered eye fluttered, then opened. Shut. She groaned.

Grabbing her hand—very gingerly—I said, "Rachel, it's me, Aldea."

She uttered a low moan filled with pain and her face tightened. Weakly, she cracked her eye open. A subconjunctival hemorrhage painted the bottom portion. "Aldea..." she whispered.

"I'm here," I said. A lump rose in my throat, and I fought the urge to cry. I rubbed my thumb across the back of her hand, providing meager comfort.

She shifted and gave a sharp yelp. "Aldea... something happened."

"I know."

Her split lip curled. "He's... not the Shawn I fell in love with." Every spoken s came out lisped. "The chip... it's the chip. I know it."

I squeezed her hand as lightly as I could, unsure if she'd suffered any injury to it. My fingers brushed against a massive ring encrusted with gore and instantly I knew what happened to Shawn's face and head: Rachel hadn't gone down without a fight.

"I'll fix this, I promise," I said.

Her eye widened and the swollen skin of her face tightened. "Behind... you," she wheezed.

As soon as her words registered, I dropped her hand and rolled, instinct guiding me. Shawn let loose a roar and his body fell where mine had been moments ago. The tile shook and I felt the vibration from his body hitting the floor.

"Stop... him," Rachel hissed. Despite her injuries, she reached for him and wrapped her arms around his naked torso, pummeling him with her right hand, the ring connecting with the back of his head. He bucked and the muscles in his back rippled, yet she hung on.

"Let go of me you fucking bitch!" Shawn screamed, his voice guttural. Rachel's fingernails clawed his back, drawing blood. "I'm so sick of your shit!" Shawn yelled. As if he'd completely forgotten about me, he turned all attention to his wife, his rage boiling over, filling the bathroom with sickly heat. Rachel clung to him like a bull rider desperately counting down eight seconds. Shawn roared, raining down blows that mostly found their mark, but they were slowed, as if his brain wasn't firing like it should.

My mind sputtered... then I remembered.

I thrust my right hand in my pocket and fingers closed around the cool metal of the hammer. Pulling it free, I hesitated; chances were, I only had one chance to hit him, and I had to make it count.

Rachel choked out, her face reddening above Shawn's thumbs wrapped around her throat, crushing her cricoid cartilage.

My eyes found his occiput—the skin split and bleeding—and it clicked. The chip gleamed under the bright bathroom lights, peeking from under a curtain of blood. Thrusting the hammer above my head, I screamed and leapt at Shawn, still utterly engrossed in throttling his wife to death. One shot. I had one shot. I brought the hammer's tip down with all my might—dead on—the impact jolting my shoulder joints so hard I momentarily worried I tore countless ligaments.

CRACK!

Shawn let out a yelp like a sickly dog. He tried to stand and stumbled. Rachel redoubled her efforts, fingers blanched bone white as she wrapped her arms around Shawn's and held on for dear life; mine.

"Again!" Rachel cried, pain lacing the word.

CRACK!

CRACK!

CRACK!

Again and again, I brought the hammer down in the same spot. More blood poured from the wound. Barely visible through the hemorrhage, I aimed for the silver chip, and I brought the hammer down one last time.

SMASH!

The chip shattered into pieces and all tone left Shawn's body. He went limp and I met Rachel's eye. A ghost of a smile stretched her lips, and then she too lost consciousness.

My chest heaved and I took a moment to catch my breath, gaping at the carnage. So much blood. All of this... because of me. Rachel trusted me, helped me even, and look where it got us. A deep ache filled my torso—a mix of devastation and shame—and I fought the urge to break into tears. If I did, I'd lose it; absolutely lose my mind. Two people I considered friends lay at my feet, possibly dying while I tried to contain my panic. Breathe. Breathe. I exhaled and shuddered. Again. Again. Once I'd calmed my racing heart, I grabbed my cellphone, noting it and my forearms were splattered with Shawn's blood—small red pearls that winked under the lights. I knew what I had to do.

I dialed 9-1-1.

"9-1-1, what's your emergency?"

I told them.

I plunged my bare fingers into Shawn's wound and removed the splintered chip, plucking each silver shard from its home. Into the toilet they went, and I flushed.

The pieces swirled down the drain, my hopes and dreams.

Just then, Shawn moaned, chilling my blood.

Fear spiked as cortisol and adrenaline dumped into my blood stream and I whirled around, still clutching the hammer. I bellowed, channeling my fear, my rage at the man who would end my life without so much as a second thought. My hubris created him after all:

Dr. Absinthe's monster.

The hammer slammed into his previously fractured temple with an audible *crunch*, and I felt the bone give way through the small instrument, the metal vibrating in my grip.

The hammer tumbled to the tile, landing with a *clink*. I stared at my trembling hands—spattered with dried and fresh blood. I took a deep breath in and tasted the iron in the air.

Then I eased my hands around Rachel's neck, holding steady pressure, mindful not to leave bruises. Minutes passed, inching along. I loosened my grip, blindly feeling with my fingertips until I felt the curve of her trachea and I located her carotid again.

Nothing.

I leaned back, wiping the back of my hand across my nose, mixing tears, snot, and blood together. My chest ached and I heaved out a sigh, feeling exhausted. Bone weary. But it wasn't over yet. The police and paramedics would be here soon.

I rolled Shawn over onto his back, ignoring his ruined skull and face and assumed the position over him: on my knees, right hand resting on my left on Shawn's chest. When I heard them breach the door, I'd start CPR. Not till then though; the CPR was most likely futile but... I wasn't going to take any chances.

Not after all this.

The monster was dead.

42

Dr. Absinthe

I CHECKED INTO THE conference, giving my name to the bored woman manning the table. "Here," the woman said flatly, handing me a name tag and a folder.

"Thanks," I answered. I didn't have clinic today—in fact, I'd cancelled all my appointments last week, still reeling from the trauma and double murder—and I'd elected to dress in jogger sweatpants and a comfy hoody. Minimal makeup. No white coat. I pulled an Adidas cap on and donned glasses instead of my usual contacts, going as incognito as possible. Some time passed but not enough to walk around brazenly as myself. When I had, whispers followed me down the halls along with looks of pity. I didn't need that right now.

Entering the conference room, I spied four carafes—two with regular coffee, one decaf, one of hot water, presumably for tea—and a tray of generic pastries. Standard fare for a CME conference. Today's topic? *Strokes and Advancements in the Field.* I didn't care about strokes; the hospital employed neurologists specifically trained to manage those patients. But I needed CMEs and I'd already accepted I'd be bored stiff the next hour.

Clutching my folder, I scanned the room, settling down on a seat in the far back. Out of sight, out of mind. Like in medical school, the brown-nosers sat front and center. I leaned back in my chair and thumbed through my phone, looking at my most recent photos, trying to take my mind off the pain coursing through me. Sadness and guilt crested whenever I gave it a chance to gain a foothold and I needed a distraction.

The first photo was Taylor standing under a tree with a glass of red wine in hand. She stared up into the branches with an expression of serene happiness. She'd held me after I gave my statement to the police, removed my soiled clothing with care, and herded me into the shower, washing away blood and gore, but not my sins. Even she didn't know about those. Listened to me sob, comforting my fears. I was insanely lucky to have her.

The next photo was of Spooky, curled up into a ball, reminding me of a Fibonacci spiral.

Another photo of Taylor and I; Taylor thrusting her recently adorned left ring finger at the camera. I smiled. I still couldn't believe she said yes. And maybe it was impulsive of me so soon after moving in together but after what happened with the Gilberts and how wonderful she'd been... I decided to live my life to the fullest; we were never guaranteed tomorrow.

"—did you guys hear what happened to Rachel?"

Yanking my head up, I looked around and found the gossiper, nestled within a group of chattering women in the seats right in front of me. Each were dressed in scrubs, and I caught a flash of a badges—Emergency Department.

"No, what?"

One of the women—a blonde with tousled curls and a vaguely pissy look on her face—leaned forward, speaking in tones she might have thought hushed. One look told me she was the type of person who fattened themselves on other's pain and suffering. She fluttered overly mascaraed eyelashes and rolled her eyes. "Where the hell have you been Aleshia? It's been all over the news! Plus, everyone's talking about it."

Aleshia—platinum blond with two rather prominent assets that probably cost a pretty penny—scoffed, "Aly, you know I don't watch the news. It's too depressing. And I did a social media cleanse recently; for my mental health."

Aly—gossiper extraordinaire—grinned. "Lucky you have me, then. I got *all* the deets." She tossed a lock of curls behind her shoulder and loudly whispered to Aleshia, "Rachel's husband fucking killed her! Can you believe it? Beat the living shit out of her. Murdered her. I can't believe you haven't heard about this!"

Aleshia answered with a shrug.

A woman with buzzed hair and a sleeve of tattoos—a fellow member of the sapphic squad if my gaydar was any indication—said, "C'mon, Aly, stop talking shit. It was a gruesome, awful thing that happened."

Aly leaned back with an offended expression. "When have you *ever* known me to talk shit? ANYWAY. Jeff was at the scene, and he told me all about it." Aly turned, glowering at the other women. "And don't you dare tell anyone that I told you. Jeff wasn't even supposed to tell me!"

The women nodded in agreement, but I had no doubt Aly/Jeff's version of the story would spread through the hospital by 5 p.m. like an antibiotic resistant bacterium; not that it was any worse than the gossip already flying about.

Aly puffed her chest out self-importantly and continued, "Jeff said it was a blood bath. Rachel's head looked like a busted-up piñata. But she got a few good licks in."

I cringed but had to admit—Aly was right. Rachel held her own.

"And get this: Dr. Absinthe came over—and killed Shawn. Rachel and her were friends or something."

I slouched in my seat and tugged the brim of my hat over my eyes.

Likely lesbian asked, "Weird... But why'd her husband kill her? He brought her food once for lunch and they seemed happy."

Another eye roll and dismissive hand flap from Aly. "Get a clue, Megan. Appearances are deceiving! It's always the 'normal' people that are the most screwed up." Aly made air quotes, reminding me of Dr. Evil in those ridiculous *Austin Powers* movies. "Who knows? Maybe Rachel was fucking someone else—maybe even Dr. Absinthe—and Shawn found out. Went psycho. Maybe Shawn was schizophrenic. Maybe Shawn smoked some bath salts and went all feral. The possibilities are endless."

I cringed... the last thing I needed was a lesbian love triangle rumor floating around. Being involved with this was bad enough. They murmured amongst themselves and although I strained, I couldn't make out what was said.

A brunette dressed in black scrubs stretched her arms up and quipped, "I'm sure they'll make a *Dateline* episode about it. The grisly murder of a nurse at the hands of her husband—a former NBA player? That's right up their alley." She giggled maliciously. "And maybe they'll interview us! We worked with Rachel, after all. We can say, 'But they seemed so normal'!"

"You know what the worst part of all this is? Other than the whole murder thing?" Aly asked, her eyes glittering with mean-spirited humor. "Now there's a hole on day shift since Rachel ate a dirt sandwich. Hopefully they don't hire a dud to replace her. Or expect us to work even harder with the same pay."

"Wow, that's super fucked up, even for you to say," Megan replied, brushing fingers along her buzzed scalp. "You're such—"

A painful whine cut through the conference room and all heads turned towards a sheepish, bespectacled man wearing an ill-fitting suit with a polka dotted bowtie. Undoubtedly a neurologist—the only specialty besides Peds who wore bowties. He winced at the sharp noise. "Sorry!" he said, fiddling with the microphone, voice nasally and high-pitched. Muffled shuffling sounds filled the air while he fussed. The gossipy nurses snickered at the man's ineptitude but let the subject of the Gilbert massacre drop. Another whine—shorter and less annoying—echoed through the conference room, followed by silence. "Is this any better?" the speaker asked.

A handful of heads nodded and some brown-noser in the front yelled, "MUCH BETTER!"

The speaker preened, reminding me of a fussy bird. "Without further ado, I'm Dr. Noon and I'm a neurologist specializing—"

I tuned him out and stared at the black fabric of my sweatpants. The events of that horrible night came roaring back. Police officers traipsing through the apartment; medics evaluating Rachel then shaking their heads slowly; the coroner bundling Shawn into a black body bag; the regret that split my heart in two.

"You did the right thing," the officer who took my statement told me, after I recounted the events of the awful evening. They took my reflex hammer into evidence and the officer chuckled. "Impressive you did it with this little guy although it looked like you had some help. Hell of an arm you got on you!" They bagged up the NBA Championship ring, whistling at all the glittering diamonds not smattered with blood.

I *did the right thing*, I told myself.

43

Dr. Absinthe

Reading Taylor's text momentarily calmed my quaking nerves and I allowed myself a small smile.

Billie brought me a coffee in my favorite mug: Ruth Bader Ginsburg flipping the bird with DISSENT. "Here you go!" she said.

I gratefully accepted the mug. Its heat warmed my palms, providing me a sense of calm. "Thanks, Billie," I said, giving her a smile.

Billie was back to her old self. Bubbly, happy, not prone to fits of rage or psychosis. No more violated restraining orders. And as a happy extra: no headaches. After the Gilbert disaster, I returned to the drawing board, spending hours poring over all my data, examining each patient's chip with a fine-toothed comb. Mrs. Combs, Mr. Reynolds, Matthew Willis, Shawn, Billie, and I'd figured out the issue—at least, I thought I had. I'd made the appropriate adjustments and called each patient and their families to check in; thus far, no personality changes or rage episodes.

Like I'd promised Rachel: I fixed it; I thought.

And here was Billie: living proof.

I eyed the steam billowing from my coffee and decided against trialing a sip just yet. Didn't feel like burning the hell out of myself before the most important day of my life.

Billie nodded and remarked, "You look great today. New duds for the big day?"

I glanced down and admired my suit. Light heather grey, personally fitted by a tailor and everything. Paired with a simple black top and matching boots—each item handpicked by Taylor who had more fashion sense in her pinky than I contained in my whole body. "Thank you! I feel like it's my first day at school and I'm showing off or something." I brushed a non-existent hair from my jacket. "To tell the truth, I'm nervous as hell," I admitted.

Billie laughed. "I'd be worried if you weren't nervous! I can't believe you're going to talk to him face to face. In person! Like... that's a huge deal."

"Tell me about it," I replied. I'd already worried about tripping and falling flat on my face, farting, or inadvertently insulting the man. Anxiety wasn't even the word for it, terror maybe?

But you've been through worse, I reminded myself.

"You're going to do great! I just know it," Billie said.

The phone on my desk rang and I picked up the receiver. "Hello?"

"Listen, tell Billie to get her ass out here because he just rolled in," Claire hissed.

I hung up. "Claire said to *get your ass out there.*"

Billie tittered. "Oh my God, oh my God, oh my God!"

Plastering my face with a smile, I said, "It's showtime."

I waited for his arrival—each second a year. I stood and smoothed out my suit for lack of anything better to do. Being seated when he came in would lend the wrong impression. Standing was better. More respectful. The man deserved a little pomp and circumstance. I eyed the table next to the door. One of my patients—a baker sporting a brand-new migraine chip and no rage episodes—prepared a bevy of goods: macarons, tiny muffins, and brownies. Brownies were his favorite; according to the *Time* magazine article I recently read.

A brisk knock at the door made me jump. God I was a nervous wreck.

"Come in!" I called out.

The door opened and two massive men in black suits, dark sunglasses, and earpieces walked in. They offered a curt nod in the way of greeting and immediately made a circuit of the office. Looking high and low for any threats, as if I'd had a machine gun secretly installed in the wall or laid land mines around my desk. They'd performed a complete sweep of the room earlier, but I supposed one couldn't be too careful, especially for a man of this caliber.

The taller of the men curtly nodded and spoke into his wrist, "All clear, send him in."

My heart raced.

He sauntered in, far more handsome than he looked on TV. His salt and pepper hair—tending towards salt these days—was cropped closely at the sides, longer on top. No embarrassing combover like the last nutjob. I admired his outfit: a gorgeous blue suit paired with a red tie. Gleaming gold cufflinks caught the overhead lights and winked. He grinned—lines bracketing intelligent eyes—displaying perfectly white and straight teeth, a trustworthy smile. "Dr. Absinthe, it's a real pleasure to meet you," he said, offering me his right hand.

I grasped it, marveling at his smooth palm. Firm grip. Returning his smile, I said, "No, sir. The pleasure is all mine."

His eyes roved around the office, seizing on the basketball signed by Shawn. "Is that from—?" he started, not bothering to finish the question. "Sorry for your loss. I used to watch him play all the time when I was younger."

"Thank you," I replied. It didn't surprise me that he knew; all the news outlets covered it, including Brooke and Drake's show who reached out for a comment I couldn't provide. Hell... Shawn was probably the reason he even heard about my chips in the first place.

He spied the baked good spread and his eyes lit up. "Are these for me?" Peering closer, frank excitement crept into his voice. "Do my eyes deceive me? I believe this is a brownie!" He laughed—a delightful timbre that immediately put me at ease.

I nodded. "Sure is! One of my other patients owns a bakery and was kind enough to provide us with this smorgasbord."

Grabbing a napkin, he loaded two brownies and a blueberry muffin on a small plate. "Don't tell my trainer or my wife I'm eating these. I'll catch hell!"

Miming zipping my lips shut, I said, "You got it. Pretty sure that falls into doctor-patient confidentiality anyway." I gestured at the chairs in front of my desk. "Please. Have a seat. Make yourself comfortable."

He sat and eagerly eyed his treats.

Coffee! He needed coffee. "Can I get you a coffee?" I asked. "We have a nice espresso machine if that's more your speed."

"No, thank you. I've already had about a gallon of the stuff today," he replied, patting his stomach. He took a bite of brownie and his eyes rolled back in his head. He sighed with supreme pleasure. "This is so good. You're going to have to get me their contact info. I'll need to procure a supplier for my secret stash."

I imagined Mrs. Steffen's pleasure when I told her he liked them. "Can do!"

He finished his brownie—looking like the cat that got the canary—and leaned back. "I must say—and this might be the baked goods talking—you might be the best damn doctor I've ever met."

I blushed and pulled his records up on my computer. "You flatterer," I said. Steepling my fingers, I leaned forward and said:

"Now, Mr. President. Let's talk about your migraines."

Acknowledgments

The idea for this book came from brainstorming sessions with Ashley who always lets me bounce ideas off her. Thanks for reading one of the first drafts and loving it!

To Fraley, my work wife/personal assistant: thank you for thoroughly picking through your copy and finding all those pesky typos/helping me refine the work.

To all my beta readers who read the first iteration; your feedback was invaluable. My boy, Nathaniel J. Darkish, my fellow word toiler kept me accountable when I didn't feel like editing.

A big thanks to my editor, Michael Dolan; without you, this would only be an idea rattling around in my brain. I value your feedback and can't wait to eat pasta with you soon.

My publisher, Winding Road Stories, who made my dreams a reality.

To my family and friends who are insanely supportive of me.

Rej, who designs the coolest covers in existence.

All my Twitter peeps who laugh at my shitty jokes/memes and encourage me (whether for good or evil).

To Theodore who sits next to me while I write and to Cat Bane who runs around screaming while I write.

And lastly, to all the DJs whose podcasts keep me company whilst I type away.

About the Author

N.J. Gallegos is an Emergency Physician by day, horror author by night. Her works include: *The Broken Heart*, *Just Desserts*, *Only You Can Prevent Forest Fires*, and *It's Me, Hi, I'm the Zombie, It's Me*, amongst many other short stories and drabbles. You can hear her sultry voice as cohost on *The Scream Kings Podcast* and when she's not writing or chatting about all things horror, she's watching reality TV, going for a run, or checking out craft beers with her wife. Check out her meme game on Twitter @DrSpooky_ER, head over to her personal website: njgallegos.com, or read her short stories at https://vocal.media/authors/n-j-gallegos.